COME SNOWFALL

A NOVEL

CINDY HIDAY

This is a work of fiction. Care was taken to depict locations and historical details of the Oregon Trail as accurately as possible, but all characters and situations in this story are fictitious. Any similarity to real persons, living or dead, is coincidental.

For Jack

Other titles by Cindy Hiday

Destination Stardust
Iditarod Nights
Her Phoenix Heart
A Bed of Roses

Chapter 1

It only took getting knocked on her butt one time to learn what she'd done wrong the day her pa taught her to shoot. Wounded her pride more than her sit-down. As Alice drew a bead on the snowshoe hare munching at the edge of the pasture, the memory of that day flashed through her thoughts. She pulled slow on the trigger of her Winchester rifle and braced for the recoil.

The shot echoed off the hill behind the ranch. The hare jumped, and Alice feared she had missed. But instead of darting away, the hare collapsed and gave a final weak kick. A clean head shot, Alice saw as she knelt beside it. She passed a hand over the animal's soft fur, felt its fading warmth. "Thank you for the life you give that I may survive," she prayed, just as

Ma taught her.

"Never take a life without good reason," Ma told her years ago. "And never forget to thank the Great Spirit for allowing you one more day of life in exchange."

Emptiness threatened to suck the strength from Alice's body: an emptiness of the heart, not of the belly. She knew how to keep herself fed decent enough, but every now and again loneliness snuck up and hit her hard in the chest. She looked across the field to a grove of aspen, where three graves rested. By her reckoning, she had nothing to thank the Great Spirit for.

Alice grabbed the hare's hind legs and made her way across the pasture toward the cabin. The summer-dried grass crunched under the soles of her boots and a light breeze off the mountains filled the air with a freshness that promised another fine day.

She rounded the back of the barn and spotted the rider a quarter mile off. She knew how far it was because Pa told her so. He always had a head for distances and figures. The rider sat long atop a handsome palomino, wore a black coat and low-crowned hat. The morning sun, already warm and sharp, caught the glint of a sidearm at the man's hip. Alice's heart quickened.

A lawman, come to take her property. No doubt hired by that snake, Mr. Pressfield, in Baker City. The chickens squawked and fluttered as Alice darted past the coup and ran for the cabin.

She tossed the hare in the wash basin and stood in the open doorway, the rifle braced across the waist of her bibbed britches, and waited as the man pulled his horse up a few feet shy of the porch. A fine-bred horse, stallion, pale golden coat, white mane and tail, head high and alert. It looked well-traveled yet able to put in more miles if called upon. A mount for emperors and Indian chiefs, her pa would say. Its rider did not dismount, but pushed his hat high on his forehead and regarded her.

A start of recognition shivered through Alice. She'd never met this man before, she was certain, yet she knew him. How was that possible?

"Is this the Bonet-Calder spread?" he asked.

"It is. State your business."

"Might you be Alice?"

She drew the rifle to her shoulder. "I said state your business, or I'll bury you where you land and sell that fine horse of yours." The palomino sidestepped and Alice followed its rider in her sights.

The man raised his arms wide at his sides. "Easy, girl. I mean you no harm."

"You've got to the count of three."

"Name's Henry Bonet," he said. "If you're Alice, I'm your Uncle Hank. I come to see my sister."

He had Ma's narrow nose and dark eyes. Raven-black hair poked out from under the brim of his hat. Here sat the older brother her ma had talked of with fondness, had missed something fierce, wrote to often. Yet not once had he heeded her pleas to come for a visit and meet the family. To Alice's way of thinking, he deserved to be shot for the disappointment he'd caused.

Nevertheless, she lowered the rifle. She would not give Pressfield reason to throw her in the county jail and take her land. Shooting her own kin would give him reason plenty. "You're too late," she said, biting the words out.

The man's shoulders lost their starch, and he lowered his arms. "How long?"

"Smallpox took her a month ago."

"And your pa?"

Alice blinked through the sudden

unwelcome tears his question brought. "He passed three days after Ma."

The man hung his head a moment, then looked up and said, "There was a boy, Joseph Calder Junior."

Little Joey. Alice swallowed hard. "He went first."

The man swore soft under his breath.

"You best be moving on," Alice told him. "Ain't nothing here for you."

"My horse needs water and a rub down," he said. "I rode him long to get here."

Alice wanted the man gone. She had a hare to dress and morning chores to tend to. But she would not deny a horse in need of attention. She jutted her chin toward the corral and watering trough. "You'll find what you want over there. Give him some of that grain in the barn, too."

"Appreciate it." He dismounted, slow and stiff like, stirring the dust from his broadcloth suit. Along with the pistol at his hip, he wore a long-blade knife and sheathe strapped to his leg.

As he led his horse to the corral, Alice set her jaw and told herself it mattered not how long the man had been in the saddle or that he was her uncle. He had not earned the right to share her grief, and she did not want his sympathy.

~~~

Hank lifted up on the corral gate, taking note of a loose hinge, led his horse inside and stripped its gear. The barn smelled of hay and leather harnesses and fresh manure. The half-dozen stalls down each side of the wide center passage looked to be empty. He fetched a scoop of grain from the bin and took it to his deserving horse. They'd been in southern Colorado when word reached him of the smallpox sweeping eastern Oregon. Unsettled by the news, Hank had pushed to get here, to assure himself that Anne and her family were safe.

The hard ride had been for naught.

He took up a handful of straw and gave his horse a rubdown. When he returned to the barn a second time, he lost his momentum and the weight of his sister's death drove him to his knees. He should have come sooner. His sister had written to him often, invited him to see their spread, to meet his baby niece. *She has her father's red hair!* Annie wrote. A few years later came news of a nephew. But there seemed to always be one more roundup, one more poker game, one more ridge to ride over. He thought
~~~

there'd be more time.

Oh, Annie. Damn it, Annie. I'm sorry.

Hank hung his head and wept.

~~~

Alice skinned and gutted the hare, all the while peering through the kitchen window for the stranger tending to his horse. Just when she thought she had a handle on her grief, up rides somebody claiming to be her uncle and looking so much like her ma it hurt.

He was kin. Maybe the only kin she had left. Pa said his folks died of cholera when he was nineteen. He sold their home in Missouri and used the money to head west. In Wyoming, he met the prettiest girl he'd ever seen, as he told it. Ma would always blush when he got to that part of the story. After a short courtship, he and that pretty girl were married and headed west together. They brought the pretty girl's mother along, Alice's grandma Ela, but Alice never got to meet her, because she drowned in a river crossing before reaching Oregon. Ma sent word to her father, still in Wyoming, about the accident but never heard back. For all anybody knew, he was dead too.

Hank, Ma's older brother by two years, left home at the age of fifteen because he and his
~~~

father didn't get along. He sent a postcard now and again, from places like California, New Mexico, Nevada, letting his sister know he was thinking of her, yet he always had one reason or another for not visiting.

Well, he was here now, and Alice didn't know what to do with him.

She laid the cleaned hare on the block and cut it into pieces for the stew pot. With potatoes and onions, she figured to get three or four meals from it. She pumped enough water into the pot to cover the pieces and set it on the front plate of the cast iron cook stove her ma had been so proud of. Pa paid a tidy sum for the J. Woodruff & Sons step-top at the hardware store in Baker City, hauled it five miles by wagon and installed it himself. Alice had been but a baby at the time, too young to remember, but her pa told the story often.

That was all she had left: this place and the stories it held. No way was Pressfield going to take it from her.

What about Ma's brother? For all she knew, he could be an outlaw, on the run from justice. It would explain his never coming around. His nice clothes and horse suggested he'd done well for himself. Had he come by it honest or by some other means? What if he expected to profit from his sister's passing? What if he should decide the ranch belonged to him?

She eyed the Winchester leaning against the pantry door. Ma taught her to stand up for herself, be the first to shoot if a man intended her harm. Alice doubted that meant shooting her own kin. But what if that kin had a notion to take —

A familiar sound at the chopping block down by the barn cut short her thoughts. *Pa!* Alice rushed to the window.

Her uncle stood at the broad, low block, and her breath hitched. *You fool. Pa's dead and buried.* Her uncle had taken his jacket off, laid it over the top rail of the corral, rolled his white shirt cuffs to his elbows. His hat rested on a post and his unkempt hair shined in the morning sun. He split another chunk of wood, then another. He swung the ax hard and fast. Every now and again, he'd stop and swipe at his face with the back of his hand.

Alice turned away. She knew what drove her uncle to attack the firewood like he meant to kill it. She could tell him it wouldn't do no good; the pain would still be there once the anger played itself out. But he'd have to realize that for himself. Just like she did.

~~~
~~~

Hank welcomed the tightness in his muscles, the solid contact of blade meeting wood, the bite of the hickory handle in his hands. He closed off his thoughts and lost himself in the physical chore. Tears gave way to sweat. If he didn't think, he didn't feel.

But soon enough, he did think. He thought about his sister, dead before he got a chance to tell her he was sorry. Her husband, Joseph, an educated man, a good father, by what Annie wrote of him in her letters. The nephew he never met. He remembered his sister said they called him Joey. And he thought about his niece, Alice, left to fend for herself, her family gone but for an uncle she did not know.

She was as much a stranger to him as he was to her. For the life of him, Hank could not remember her age. Eleven? Twelve? The girl who met him at the door, rifle in hand, her long red hair braided the way Annie use to wear hers, was hardly a child, but she had not yet begun to fill out. At least not from what he could tell by the over-sized man's clothes she wore. He recalled Annie writing that her daughter wanted nothing to do with dresses and had an independent streak to be reckoned with. *She got her father's looks, but her temperament reminds me of you,* Annie wrote.

If that was true, Hank had a hunch she wouldn't take kindly to the notion of him hanging around. He didn't care much for the notion himself. He'd been a drifter for over half his life. Staying in one place long wasn't in his nature.

But a ranch this size was too much for one person to handle, especially somebody who barely stood as tall as the rifle she packed around. He'd noticed a handful of foals in the pasture, some grazing alongside their mothers, others frisking up their hooves and challenging their balance. The bay mare in the paddock, her belly hanging low and her tail relaxed, looked ready to give birth in a matter of days. Unless the Calder family had taken ill before breeding season, many of the mares in the pasture were already pregnant again, which meant the work would multiply next spring.

But first there was winter to get through. Situated at the foothills of the Blue Mountain Range, the area no doubt got its share of snow. The horses would have to be hand fed, the chickens kept warm, firewood stocked. What kind of food stores had been put up?

Hardship may have aged Alice ahead of her years, but she was still just a girl. His sister's girl. Like it or not, he couldn't just ride away.

~~~

"I don't need nobody lookin' after me," Alice stated as she slopped coffee into her uncle's cup and onto his work-rough hand.

He made no mention of it, swiped his hand dry on his pant leg and took a sip. "That's some fine coffee."

Alice wasn't going to be done in by his compliment, not after he invited himself to have a sit-down before she could say otherwise. He'd be on his way as soon as his horse had a rest. She'd see to it. She poured herself a cup, returned the pot to the back plate of the cook stove, and added another stick of wood to the firebox before returning to the table. "I know how to take care of myself."

"No doubt you do, but it's not good, you living here alone. There's too much for a girl your age to handle. How old are you?"

"Twelve, almost thirteen." Then in case he hadn't heard her the first half dozen times, she said, "I'm managing just fine."

"How many horses have you got?"

"Twenty-three, last count." Could be more. Alice suspected there were a few holed up in a draw south of the ranch that she hadn't gotten to yet.
~~~

"You've been tending them on your own?"

"I've got neighbors...the widow Nan and her two boys...they come over and help out from time to time."

"Running a spread like this has expenses," her uncle said.

Alice had found her folks' stash under the floorboards in their bedroom. It didn't amount to much. If she could find somebody to buy the saddle-broke horses...

"I'll make do." She did not care for the raised-brow look her uncle aimed at her over the rim of his coffee cup, like he questioned the truth of her words. Well she didn't trust him either. "I didn't ask you to come, and I didn't ask for your help."

"No, you did not. But I'm here now. We're kin. Kin looks after each other."

"Like you looked after your sister." Alice regretted her remark the instant she spoke it. Ma always told her to mind her smart mouth, that it could get her into trouble some day, or cause a body hurt. She saw by the tight look on her uncle's face, she had caused him hurt. The man purely had her confused, wanting to shoot him one minute and worrying over his feelings the next. "That was uncalled for," she said by way of an apology.

"But deserved." He pushed his empty cup across the table. "Got any more of that fine coffee?"

Alice refilled his cup.

"Thank you kindly."

She gave a nod, checked on the stew pot and moved it to a back plate to keep it from boiling over. "Don't you have a home of your own somewhere to tend to?" she asked, her back to him.

"That palomino and what's in my saddlebags is everything I own."

Alice rounded on him. "And this ranch is all I own. Ain't nobody takin' it from me."

"I don't want your ranch, girl." He drew in a long breath. "I'll make you a deal."

"What kind of deal?"

"You need another pair of hands to help out around here," he said. "And I've got a debt to pay."

Alice snorted. "If you're thinking you've got some inheritance comin' – "

"Nothing like that."

"I ain't sellin' this place to pay off a debt I had nothing to do with," Alice persisted.

Her uncle shook his head. "I'm not talking about a money debt. I have a debt to Annie, your ma. It's *her* I owe. The only way to pay up now that she's gone is to see after her girl as best I can."

"You said yourself you ain't got much."

He gave her a crooked smile. "Indeed I did. You do have your ma's sass."

Alice folded her arms across her chest. "I take that as a compliment."

"As well you should. You're right, I don't have much, but I set aside a small cache that'll keep us afloat for a while. Plus I've got two good hands and a strong back."

Mention of a cache caused Alice pause. Was it enough to make Pressfield back off and leave her be? Even if it wasn't, the presence of her uncle on the property may make the snake think twice about getting too close.

As much as Alice hated to admit it, the day-to-day chores it took to keep the ranch going were more than she could manage. And it wasn't fair to rely on her neighbors to always take up the slack. They had their own place to run, made harder after Nan's husband died two winters ago.

Alice returned to the table and took a seat across from her uncle. "What do you know about horses?"

"I spent some time on a breeding ranch a few years back. That's where I come by the palomino."

Alice thought of the bay yet to drop her foal, and the other mares set to foal next spring. An extra pair of hands would assure they'd be tended to proper. "You know your way around an ax. How are you at mending fences?"

"Done my share." He gave a nod at the stove. "And I know how to make that rabbit into a proper stew."

Alice huffed. "I can make stew."

"Not the way I make it."

He had her attention. She could feed herself, but most times it didn't come out as nice as Ma's. If he took over the cooking, she'd have more time for other chores. Lest her uncle get any ideas about moving in just because he was family, she said, "You ain't sleepin' in the house."

"I saw a cot and potbelly stove in the barn that'll do me fine."

"If it don't work out, you'll be on your way. No hard feelings."

"No hard feelings."

Alice reached across the table to shake his hand. "You got yourself a deal."

Chapter 2

Hank released Alice's hand at the sound of a rider approaching.

"That'll be Nan," his niece said.

A tall woman in a spring-blue dress brushed through the cabin door, the color high on her cheeks. Some of her soft yellow hair had worked free of the bun at the back of her neck, like she'd ridden at a good clip.

A handsome woman, Hank thought. But she saw him sitting there, across the table from Alice, and gave him a look that could sour milk. He stood and smiled, hoping to soothe the woman's concern. "Good morning, ma'am. I'm Henry Bonet."

That drew her up short. No doubt she'd heard the name before. He couldn't see that it sweetened her disposition any.

"You would be Anne's brother then," she said.

"Yes, ma'am."

She gave a curt nod. "I'm Mrs. Trevor. I own the ranch north of here."

"Pleased to meet you, Mrs. Trevor."

She did not return the sentiment, eyed him a moment longer with open distrust, then brushed by him to hand Alice a covered mason jar. "You'll want to put this in the cellar right away."

The contents looked to be fresh-churned butter. Hank's mouth fairly watered at the sight of it.

"Thank you," Alice said. She took the jar and turned to him. "You're standing on the cellar door."

Hank stepped aside and lifted on the latch ring set in the floor, revealing a ladder to the dirt cellar. Nan Trevor stood with her hands folded at her skirt and kept an eye on him, while Alice climbed down then back up moments later, the pockets of her over-sized britches stuffed with potatoes and a couple large onions cradled in the crook on one arm.

"I'll send Jacob over later to chop stove wood," Mrs. Trevor told the girl.

"No need," Hank said. "I took care of it."

It was clear the woman did not want to leave Alice alone as long as he was there. Nothing he could do about that, but he could give them a minute to talk private. "If you'll excuse me." He took up his hat and stepped outside.

A sturdy buckskin stood hitched to the porch railing, and Hank wondered if the Trevors raised horse stock as well. It was good country for it. The surrounding mountains fed the forks of the Powder River and formed a fertile valley, ripe for settlers to build a life on. His sister and her husband had chosen their piece of land well. If a man were of a mind to settle down, Hank could think of none better.

The door closed and Nan Trevor stepped up beside him. "Alice tells me you plan to sleep in the barn."

"That was our agreement."

"The nights get bitterly cold here in the winter."

He heard the question in her comment. *How long do you intend to stay?* "Won't be the first cold night I've slept outdoors, but thank you for your concern."

Her lips thinned.

"You best speak your mind, ma'am, seeing as how we both have that girl's safe keeping to heart."

"Do you, Mr. Bonet? It's very convenient, you showing up here when the child has nobody to fend for her and all this land to be had."

It was his turn to be caught up short. "Has someone threatened to take the ranch?"

"Not in so many words. But Mr. Pressfield, president of the bank in Baker City, claims Joseph Calder owed him money. Whether he intends to put a lien on this place as payment, I do not know."

"How much did Calder owe?"

"I didn't feel it my place to ask Alice to show me her father's ledger. But Joseph was a dreamer, and I know there were times it worried on Anne."

"Thank you for being straight with me. As I told Alice, I came hoping to see my sister, nothing more."

"I am sorry for your loss. Anne was a good person and my friend. It isn't easy, finding another woman in these parts to converse with." She looked up at him. She had pretty green eyes. "What will you do now, Mr. Bonet?"

"Stay and see after what's left of my family."

She seemed satisfied with his answer, or

resigned, for she nodded and started down the steps to her horse.

"You are wrong about one thing, Mrs. Trevor."

She turned, a frown drawing her brows close.

"Alice has had someone fending for her long before I got here," he said. "I am in your debt."

Her frown eased. "There is no debt to be paid. Alice is like a daughter to me."

He caught the warning in her voice and respected it. "At least let me pay for the butter."

"Cordelia is Alice's cow. We're keeping it at our place to ease her burden. Our cow died last year and we've got the room. But if you'd like its return – "

"I'll abide by whatever deal you made with my niece. I never was much for milking."

Nan Trevor allowed a brief smile at this, and Hank suddenly found the prospect of hanging around easier to consider. "Cordelia's a mighty big name for a milk cow," he said.

"You haven't read Shakespeare, I take it."

"No, ma'am. There weren't many books where I've been."

"Alice will explain, if she's a mind to." Nan mounted her horse. "Good day to you, Mr.

Bonet."

"Good day, Mrs. Trevor."

~~~

Alice stood at the butcher block chopping onions, tears rolling down her cheeks. Hank hung his hat on a peg by the door and took the knife from her. "Go splash cold water on your face," he said. "It cuts the sting some."

It was clear by the girl's scowl she did not care for being told what to do, but she didn't argue. She worked the pump handle over the wash tub and stuck her face under the water.

Hank finished the onions and started on the potatoes. "Do you have any mint?" he asked.

Alice stared at him, water dripping down the front of her shirt. "Mint?"

"Green, kinda peppery tasting – "

"I know what mint is," she snapped. "What do you want it for?"

"The stew." Hank winked, hoping to lighten her mood a touch. "It's my secret ingredient."

She stared at him a moment longer, a stricken look on her face. "That's how Ma use to make the stew so special," she said, her voice gone small.

The pain he saw in her eyes tore at him.
~~~

She'd been through more than a girl her age ought to have, that was for damn sure. "We learned it from our mother," he told her, and turned back to chopping.

Alice set a jar of dried mint leaves beside him.

"Put a couple pinches in the pot," Hank told her. "Then make up a list of supplies you need. I'm riding into town tomorrow."

"I'm going with you."

Hank did not contradict the girl. He would leave her at the mercantile to gather the things on her list, while he paid Mr. Pressfield a visit. But first he needed to get a look at Joe Calder's ledger, find out what his debt to the bank president had been for.

~~~

Alice took a mouthful of rabbit stew. It tasted like Ma made it, and tears came to her eyes. It worried on her that she'd forgotten the secret ingredient. She wanted to remember everything about her family, hold on fiercely to her memories of them. She chanced a look at her uncle sitting across the table, afraid he might have caught her crying, but he seemed intent on the contents of his own bowl, spoon in one callused hand, a half-eaten biscuit slathered with butter in the other. He'd
~~~

combed his hair and washed up before sitting at the table, just like Ma always told her to do. Alice wondered if it was a habit their own mother had taught them. What manner of things did her uncle remember about his kin, *her* kin, that she could learn from?

"Mrs. Trevor tells me you read Shakespeare," he said without looking up.

"I read him some," Alice replied. "But I favor James Fenimore Cooper, *The Deerslayer*, *The Last of the Mohicans*. Pa was big on reading."

"You're lucky. An education is important."

A memory of Pa helping Ma learn words from the pages of the *Bedrock Democrat* newspaper, teaching her to study the price of goods and to write letters, came to Alice's mind. Ma said she'd seen little of the inside of a schoolhouse as a child. What of Uncle Hank? There were the postcards he'd sent, but he could have had somebody else do the writing for him. Alice asked, "Do you read, Uncle?"

He looked up, nodded. "I can read, though I'm sorry to say the books you mention are beyond me."

"Pa has a whole shelf of books in his room," Alice said. "If you've a mind to study them, I could bring them out some time."

"I'd like that. Thank you. I'd like to learn

why you gave your milk cow such a fine name."

Cordelia. The favorite daughter of a king. Alice smiled. "Then that's the book we'll study on first." She went back to eating her stew, pleased at the thought of having someone to share her love of stories with again.

"Are you good at numbers, too?" her uncle asked.

Alice shook her head. "I've tried, but I can't make sense of it, percentages and dividing a thing into parts that're all the same. I can add and subtract if you give me a pencil and paper, but Pa, he could do those things in his head."

"Maybe I can help you there," Uncle Hank said. "I'm pretty good with numbers."

"How is it you're good with numbers, but you can't read well?"

"I suppose for the same reason you can read well but don't know much about numbers," her uncle replied. "Not everybody's brain works the same. Partly it depends on what a person needs to rely on to get by. There was more use for numbers in the things I did over the years, than in knowing a lot of fancy words on a page."

Alice thought of the ledger in her folks' room. She surely would like to know what all it was trying to tell her. She had wanted to ask Nan for help but was embarrassed to admit her shortcoming. She'd like to know if Pressfield's claims held any water.

Alice met her uncle's gaze. She would have to put her trust in him, trust him to do right by her. The idea did not make her as uneasy as it had when he first cast a shadow at her door. "You've got yourself another deal," she said.

~~~

After they'd eaten, Hank helped Alice clear the table and wash dishes. With her red hair and over-sized man's clothes, the girl resembled his sister hardly at all, yet Hank saw Annie tucked away in a gesture, a mannerism. It was easy for his mind to wander back to a time when he had done chores with Annie at his side, just as he and Alice did now.

Alice stacked the blue enameled bowls on a shelf to one side of the cook stove. Annie had always been partial to blue. He use to pick her bunches of coyote mint and bluebells to take her mind off their father's drunkenness.

"I'll get Pa's ledger," Alice said, breaking into his thoughts.

"If it's alright with you, I'd like to visit my sister's grave first."

~~~

His niece led him to a grassy rise a short walk from the house. A grove of aspen bordered the family plot. Hank removed his hat as they approached the three resting spots facing west, each with a carved wooden marker. The smallest, Joseph Calder Jr., lie between Joseph Calder Sr. and Anne Calder. Below his sister's Christian name was her Arapaho name: She Is Quiet. Seeing it squeezed at Hank's heart.

"I didn't know how to spell it in Arapaho," Alice said, as if to apologize.

"Nor do I," Hank admitted. "It's a complicated language. Speaking it is beyond me, as well." It did not help that he had resisted his mother's attempts to teach him.

The girl said something that sounded distantly familiar, *"Teneiitooneiht,"* but Hank had been away from the language too long to correct her if she misspoke.

"Did Annie tell you the story behind her given name?" he asked.

Alice bent and picked a leaf from her brother's grave. "She said she was good at being real quiet, so as not to disturb her father. She said he got angry if he was disturbed."

Angry was too mild a word to describe their father's drunken rages, but the girl did not need to know more than Annie had chosen to tell her. "Your ma was also good at quieting me when I refused to listen to anybody else."

"They called you Storm Coming."

Hank gave a wry smile at the memory. "Mother said a storm of unhappiness followed me wherever I went."

His niece looked up at him. "Why?"

A rancid lump churned in Hank's stomach. It was a question he'd asked himself many times. He always came back to the same answer. "I must have been born with my father's anger in me."

Alice huffed. "Or maybe you just want folks to believe that, so you've got an excuse to keep your distance." She turned abruptly and started back to the cabin without waiting for a response.

Hank did not try to stop her. He didn't expect her to forgive him for staying away. Not when he wouldn't forgive himself. He walked to the creek to pick flowers for his sister's grave.

~~~

When Hank returned to the cabin, Alice had a fresh pot of coffee boiling and a ledger bound in cowhide laid out on the table. She glanced his way and took another cup from the
~~~

shelf. She was a young girl trying to fill her parents' shoes, her thin body swallowed up in her pa's clothes, her frizzed red hair coming loose from its braids. He said the only thing he could, "I'm sorry, Alice. I want you to know that."

She nodded and handed him a cup of coffee.

They sat at the table and Hank opened the ledger. It took him a bit to get a handle on Joseph Calder's method of recording purchases and expenses, but once he did, he could see that Mr. Daniel J. Pressfield was indeed owed a sum of money to be paid upon the sale of three horses, at the price of $200 each, to the Grier and Kellogg Livery Stable. The transaction should have taken place weeks ago, most likely around the time the family fell ill.

"Did your pa tell you about the horses he planned to sell in town?" Hank asked.

"Three good saddle horses for the livery," Alice confirmed. "I helped break 'em in. When Pa got sick, Mr. Kellogg bought from a rancher south of here instead. It purely upset Pa, but there wasn't anything he could do about it, being laid up like he was. What does that have to do with Pressfield?"

Hank couldn't find a reason for Joe Calder

to borrow such a sum of money. Entries for feed and supplies to keep the ranch operating came nowhere near close to that amount. Whatever deal he'd struck with the bank's president, it had gone unrecorded. Whether deliberate or an oversight, he couldn't say.

"I don't know," he told his niece. "But I intend to find out tomorrow."

Chapter 3

Alice slept fitful. Little Joey didn't mumble to himself under the covers of the narrow bed across from hers, making up stories about cowboys and Indians. In his stories, the Indians always won. There were no soft sounds of Ma and Pa whispering to each other in the adjoining room. No rumbles and snorts from Pa. "Snored like a bear," as Ma told it. Alice use to groan and huff over all the noise her family made, sure it was intended to keep her awake.

But the silence was worse. Much worse.

She drew into a ball beneath the patchwork quilt she had helped her ma with, remembered her childish impatience over the endless squares she had been instructed to trace and cut out. If the pattern slipped in the tracing, that's the way she cut it, resulting in a lopsided patch that made getting the pieces to lie flat when stitched together all the more difficult. Alice heard her ma's sigh of disappointment like a chill breath up her back that no quilt could warm.

Each bed on the place had its own quilt, the pieces cut from clothes no longer decent to wear, each piece a memory. Even the cot in the barn. Alice wondered if her uncle realized it was his sister's handiwork that kept him warm.

True to his claim, her uncle tended the horses with the ease of a man who had done his share of wrangling, setting out grain, grooming, mucking stalls. There'd been no need to tell him to do a thing but once, if that. Feeding the chickens, collecting eggs. Watering the vegetable garden. The afternoon and evening chores went by quick, as if her own pa worked by her side.

But the man sleeping in the barn wasn't Pa. Never again would Ma's fingers work magic with a sewing needle. And a little boy's stories of cowboys and Indians were silenced forever.

An ember popped in the cook stove. Alice flinched, and tears rolled down her face.

~~~

The mid-morning sun warmed Hank's shoulders and painted the eastern mountains a
~~~

soft yellow against a sky blue enough to hurt the eyes. Pine and juniper scented the air, more alluring than any lady's fine perfume. A man could almost forget his worries in a country such as this. There was an ease in his palomino's steps that Hank had not felt in weeks, as if he and his horse were in agreement.

"Horse biscuits!"

Alice's outburst broke into Hank's rambling thoughts. He looked over at her riding next to him on a spirited young chestnut she called Penny. "Something wrong?"

"I left my list back at the cabin."

Hank winked and pulled the slip of paper from an inside pocket. "Lucky for you I spied it."

She took the paper and mumbled a thanks, tucked it into the pocket of an oversized broadcloth coat that Hank guessed had been her pa's. The weariness in the girl's face troubled him. She no doubt got about as much sleep as he did, which was next to none. Not that the cot had been uncomfortable, better than most he'd stretched out on in his life. And the soft, homemade quilt wrapped around him bested his dusty old saddle roll any day.

It was the loss they shared and the difficult

situation they found themselves in that kept Hank tossing with grief and indecision all the long night. Alice had proven her know-how when it came to running the ranch, and she had a way with horses he'd seen the likes of only once before, a Mexican fellow in Colorado who could calm the testiest beast with a touch and soft word. But the girl was too young to shoulder the responsibility she'd been saddled with. And nobody had ever accused Hank Bonet of taking responsibility for much of anything.

"You ever hear the saying 'caught between a rock and a hard place'?" he asked.

Alice shot him a look. "It's from Homer's Odyssey."

"Is that so?" Hank had never given thought to how the saying got its start.

"Odysseus and his shipload of men have to find a way between a whirlpool that could drown them, that being the hard place, and a cliff, that being the rock, where a six-headed, man-eating monster lived."

"What did they do?"

Alice appeared to study her thoughts a second before answering. "Near as I remember, there was an island with these sirens, creatures that could disguise themselves as beautiful women. I think the island was the only safe way to get around the whirlpool and the cliff. But if the men on the ship heard the sirens calling, they'd be tempted to sail right into the whirlpool to get to them. Odysseus had himself tied to the ship 'cause he wanted to hear the sirens, then he told his men to put wax in their ears so they couldn't hear a thing. That's how they sailed around the island and passed the whirlpool without getting sucked in, and Odysseus got to hear the sirens' song."

"What about the cliff monster?"

"It ate six men when they got too close, one for each of the monster's heads."

Taken aback, Hank said, "Odysseus got around the rock and a hard place by sacrificing six of his own men?"

Alice shrugged. "That's the way the story goes."

"What kind of stories are they teaching you in school?"

"It's from one of Pa's books. I don't go to school."

"Baker City doesn't have a schoolhouse?"

"It does," Alice replied, her tone curt. "But I kept getting kicked out for fighting."

Hank's gut tightened. He suspected the answer to his next question but asked anyway.

"What were the fights over?"

Alice tilted her chin in the air and stated, "I didn't like the way some of the boys teased me about being a half-breed." She looked at him. "Ma said she didn't see much of the inside of a schoolhouse as a girl either. I guess you'd know a thing or two about that."

"I would."

She accepted his blunt answer with a nod.

A speckled grouse stirred in the brush off to their left. In one slick motion, Alice pulled up her horse, drew her rifle from its boot, took aim and fired. The grouse flew into the trees and the filly danced backwards into the packhorse, making any chance at a second shot a waste of ammunition. Alice sighed. "That would have been nice for supper."

"We'll get it on the way back," Hank said.

She slid her rifle into its boot. "You don't have to come back with me, you know. If you're feeling caught between a rock and a hard place, you can just move on when we reach town." She cast him a quick glance and added, "I figure that's why you asked."

The girl was wise for her years. It made Hank uncomfortable, but he answered her honest. "You figure wrong."

"All right then." Alice kicked her impatient

horse into a trot.

They rode on in silence, Hank beset by memories of fist fights he got into as a kid, a *redskin* who dared to show himself in a white school, the beatings he took when he came home with a bloody nose, his books torn and trampled, his father calling him an ignorant half-breed, as he delivered another blow. It didn't take long to realize there was no place for a kid like him except what he could make for himself. His mother had been right to send him away.

Hank cut a sidelong look at his niece. Arapaho blood ran through her veins too. She'd already felt its sting. He'd do what he could to set things right by her. But the story she told gnawed at his conscience. He knew it for a fable, but most fables began from a place of truth. What, or who, would end up being sacrificed in finding a way through the rock and hard place they were in?

~~~

Baker City made Alice jittery inside. Too many people gathered together in too small a space. Yet at the same time, she marveled at the men's bowler hats and the ladies' colorful dresses, their wearers bustling about like bees in a hive. And she enjoyed peering through the
~~~

plate glass windows at the sundries.

She didn't need much in the way of supplies. Nan and her boys had seen to that. But judging by the amount of biscuits and coffee Uncle Hank helped himself to yesterday and again at breakfast, she figured it wise to stock up on flour and coffee beans. Maybe she'd treat herself to a piece of the imported chocolate Mrs. Henderson kept out of reach high on a back shelf. If there was money enough. Alice could not abide the thought of running a tab and being indebted to old biddy Henderson, even if it meant going without.

"Where can I find Mr. Pressfield?" Uncle Hank asked.

Alice jutted her chin down the street. "That two-story building on the right is the bank. That's where he has his office."

"And the mercantile?"

"Over there," she said, pointing to a broad, white-washed building with huge, lettered windows flanking double doors.

"You take the packhorse," her uncle said. "I'll meet you at the store directly."

"But I – "

"This is something I best handle on my own."

Truthfully, Alice had no desire to be in the

same room with Pressfield. The man sweated too much, and his eyes went where they had no business going. "If you're sure you don't need me..."

"I don't expect this to take long," Uncle Hank said, and rode on down the street without so much as a backward glance.

Alice pulled up to Henderson's Mercantile and dismounted. She looped Penny's and the packhorse's reins over the hitching rail, next to a strawberry roan sporting a worn trail saddle and bed roll, and stomped up the steps. A bell over the door tinkled as she went inside; the sweet smell of the candy counter made her stomach rumble.

Mr. Henderson and a slim man in a cowboy hat were off in one corner, looking over a display of shirts. Mrs. Henderson stood behind the counter, a white apron tied across the middle of a yellow gingham dress straining at its seams, her frazzled nut-brown hair pulled into a tight bun at the back of her head. She took one look at Alice and her mouth puckered like she'd bit into a chokecherry.

"My word, child, what are you wearing?"

~~~

In all his drifting, Hank had never ventured west of the Snake River until now.
~~~

He'd heard tell of gold in Griffin Gulch to the south. Miners from the boomtown of Auburn headed north along the Oregon Trail into Baker Valley for gold and assay supplies. Before long, Baker City came into its own as a center of commerce. It was still young: a dirt main street lined by boardwalks, a saloon at the corner, a mercantile, hotel, and livery.

Hank knew it wouldn't be long before the railroad reached the valley, at which time the population would expand, bringing with it more businesses, more government. Right now though, Baker City was a quiet, passable town. No one paid him much mind as he hitched his horse in front of the bank and entered through the tall glassed doors.

Hank had seen Pressfield's kind before: bearded and paunchy, stuffed behind a desk as pompous as its owner. Were it not for the man's influence as bank president, Hank would have considered him foolish and not worth the time. Bigwigs often struck him in that manner, with their high silk hats and Prince Albert frock coats. He disliked the man at first sight. But for Alice's sake, he forced himself to be civil.

"My name is Henry James Bonet. I am Alice Calder's uncle."

Pressfield didn't bother to stand, but gestured to one of the seats facing his desk. "What can I do for you, Mr. Bonet?"

Hank sat. "I understand Alice's father, Joseph Calder, owed you the sum of six hundred dollars."

"Owes. Death does not dismiss the debt."

Hank studied the man's close-set eyes and greased hair. "As Alice Calder's closest remaining relative, I take responsibility for her financial affairs. How did my sister's husband come to incur this debt?"

"We had a business agreement, the details of which do not concern you," Pressfield replied.

"They do if you expect to see your money," Hank said with a calm he did not feel. The man's condescending airs deserved to be knocked into the next county, and Hank was more than willing to provide the service. Once he had the answers he needed.

"Very well. Joe Calder took out a loan to invest in railroad stock. I purchased a hundred shares in his name, but he fell ill and died before the loan could be repaid."

Hank didn't know much about such things, but with the growth railroads were seeing now days, it seemed a good investment.

"Why not keep the stock for yourself as payment?" he asked.

"For my ownership to be valid, I need the signature of Calder or his beneficiary."

"Which would be Alice."

"Precisely. However, she has refused to heed my requests to come to the office, and she threatens to shoot anyone I send to the ranch to conduct business."

"She believes you mean to take the ranch from her."

Pressfield scoffed. "I am a businessman, Mr. Bonet. I have no interest in owning a horse ranch. But if I did, I would not be doing business with Miss Calder."

"Why's that?"

"Before he passed, Joseph Calder signed the deed to his property over to Mrs. Arthur Trevor."

Nan owns the ranch? "Is Alice aware of this?"

"You'll have to ask her."

Hank could no longer tolerate the stale air in the room, or this man. "I'll make you a deal, Mr. Pressfield. I will pay the six hundred dollars, for which you will issue a receipt, and you will hand possession of the railroad stock over to my niece."

"She must be present before I release possession."

"I will see to it."

"And the sum is no longer six hundred dollars. Joseph Calder agreed to pay the balance within thirty days or incur an additional twenty-six percent interest, compounded daily. The total due as of this morning is twelve hundred thirty dollars and sixty-two cents."

Hank did not have that kind of money.

"Or," Pressfield continued, "Alice Calder can sign the railroad stock over to me and I will consider the matter settled."

Something in the man's eyes didn't set right with Hank. How much was that railroad stock worth? Enough to inflate Calder's debt to the point that Pressfield gained ownership of it by default?

Either way, Pressfield won and Alice lost.

Hank stood. "Good day, Mr. Pressfield." He did not offer his hand, nor did the bank president. "You will be hearing from me again soon."

Chapter 4

"Now, Esther," Mr. Henderson said from across the store, "don't start on the girl."

"Girl?" Mrs. Henderson squawked. The woman reminded Alice of a chicken in the midst of laying an egg. "Is there a girl under all that?"

"Esther..."

Alice marched up to the counter. She liked Mr. Henderson, but she didn't need anybody fighting her fights for her. "It's all right, sir, I don't pay no mind. Everybody's entitled to their opinion, even if it doesn't make much sense."

Mrs. Henderson's ample bosom lifted. "Don't get sassy with me, young lady."

Alice grinned. "So you do admit I'm a girl." She heard Mr. Henderson stifle a snort.

Old biddy Henderson's jaw flapped, but before she could get a word out, the cowboy tossed two gray work shirts onto the counter and said, "I'll take these."

Collecting herself, Mrs. Henderson said, "Certainly," all business like.

Alice released a breath, relieved to have the woman's attention off her for the time it took the cowboy's purchases to be tallied and wrapped.

On the way to his office at the back of the store, Mr. Henderson leaned in close and whispered, "If you need my help, give a shout." His breath smelled of licorice mint.

Alice's smile was genuine this time. They both knew she'd be needing no help, but she thanked him all the same. He disappeared into the back, and she let her gaze drift to the high shelf where the box of imported chocolate bars occupied a space overlooking the entire store.

Pa had surprised her and Joey and even Ma each with a bar of their own last Christmas. He'd never had much taste for chocolate himself, he told them, but he took pleasure in watching on as his family tore at the wrappers and took their first bites. Alice saw it in his face, the way his eyes sparkled and his smile stretched as wide as the Powder River.

Remembering ached through her. She blinked and looked away.

The cowboy picked up his shirts wrapped in brown paper and tied with string, turned and tipped his broad-brimmed hat to Alice. He was younger than she'd thought at first glance, and her cheeks warmed.

"Ma'am," he said, and gave her a wink before leaving the store.

Alice watched him head for the strawberry roan. Did he live around here, or was he just passing through?

Mrs. Henderson cleared her throat and Alice cringed. She turned and faced the woman scowling at her from behind the counter. Drawing in a long sigh, Alice pulled the list from her pocket.

~~~

Hank knew the quickest place to get information was the local watering hole. He hoped to pick up any talk that might be circulating about the railroad and the going price for shares in its stock. He'd like to know what folks in these parts thought of their bank president, as well.

But a saloon was no place to take Alice. He could ride back to the cabin with her and return to town later, but that would eat up half
~~~

a day, hours better spent mending the busted gate hinge to the corral, tending to things that had started to decline since Joe Calder's death. The girl had already proven her ability to look out for herself. He'd just have to trust she didn't think he was trying to run out on her.

He saw her tying a bag of goods to the packhorse when he rode up to the mercantile. He dismounted and held the bag steady while she secured it with a couple neat half-hitches. "You get everything on your list?" he asked.

"Near enough." She turned away as if something she had no mind to discuss troubled her. "You ready to ride?"

"I'm going to stick around here awhile longer," he said. "You go on ahead and I'll catch up shortly."

The fear and anger all tangled together in her eyes stopped Hank's heart for a beat. "I meant what I said before," she told him, her voice as tight as her half-hitches. You don't have to come back if – "

"It's not like that," he said, his tone harsher than intended. "If I'm not back by the time the sun reaches that western peak, you haul out your Winchester and come looking for me, got it?"

She frowned. "What're you fixin' to do?"

"Get some answers."

"You find out anything from that snake Pressfield?"

"Some, but not enough."

She thought on his words for a second or two, her eyes on him like she was trying to read his mind, trying to decide whether or not to trust him. Then she drew in a deep breath and said, "Don't you get yourself killed."

"Wasn't planning on it."

~~~

The saloon was like any other Hank had been in, cleaner than some, the air heavy with the smell of tobacco and whiskey. A potbelly stove sat in the middle of the establishment, a long bar on one side and four tables on the other, all of them empty at this time of day but for two men at the one farthest from the door. The piano against the back wall sat quiet.

Hank stepped up to the bar and ordered coffee. The bartender was a stout man, big across the shoulders like he'd done his share of hard work in his time, but thickening in the waist like he'd been away from it for a while. He wiped a hand across the towel he had tucked in his belt as a sort of apron, produced a cup from under the bar and set it in front of Hank. "Coffee's on the stove there. Help
~~~

yourself."

Hank filled his cup and returned to the bar. The man behind it sized him up. "You'd be kin to Anne Calder, I reckon."

"Shows, does it?"

The bartender chuckled. "There is a resemblance. Also saw you ride in with the Calder girl."

"Name's Hank Bonet. Did you know my sister?"

"Only in passing. She was a hard woman not to notice. I went out to their ranch once, did some horse trading with Joe. The missus served me a cup of coffee." He shook his head. "Sad affair, the family going that way and leaving the girl on her own. You come to take her away?"

"Got no place to take her," Hank said. "We'll be staying and making a go of it here."

The bartender nodded. "Baker City's a good little town. And that's a nice piece of land Joe and his wife laid claim to. Too much for that girl to handle on her own. But now you're here, maybe she stands a chance."

"My niece knows more about ranching than I do," Hank admitted. "But I'm willing to learn." He drank his coffee. Strong, but not burnt like coffee left to sit too long on the stove could get. He appreciated that and took another drink before commencing. "I hear the railroad will make it this direction before long."

"A lot of folks are looking forward to it. Myself? I'd like to see Baker City stay just the way it is. But there's no stopping progress." He gave a shrug. "I could use the business, won't deny it. I just wish I'd had the sense to buy stock in that progress before the price jumped outta reason."

"What's it going for nowadays?"

"Last I heard it was near twenty dollars a share."

Hank allowed a soft whistle. Joseph Calder had been a forward-thinking man, bought a hundred shares of the future. A hundred shares worth about twenty thousand dollars now, and Pressfield wanted to buy them for twelve hundred and change. Alice had Pressfield pegged right; the man was a snake. Hank decided it didn't much matter what the rest of the town thought of their bank's president.

He took a minute to refill his cup and returned to the bar.

"Yes sir," the bartender went on, "folks who bought in early stand to do mighty good for themselves."

"Wouldn't mind getting in on that myself," Hank commented, "but a drifter like me doesn't have that kind of money to throw around."

"I noticed the horse you rode up on," the bartender said. "Looks like it can run."

"It's gotten me out of a pinch or two. Your point?"

"There's a race in town this Saturday. With a horse such as that, a man stands a chance at growing his purse."

Hank had never raced the palomino, but he'd told it true that he had outrun anything on four legs chasing after them. And there had been a few. "Who do I see about entering?" he asked.

The bartender tossed a look at the back table. "That'd be Doc Hatcher, in the gray vest."

Hank laid coin on the bar. "Thanks for your time."

Alice had almost finished plucking the second grouse when her uncle rode in. Relief washed through her and she nearly rushed to greet him. But anger won out and she stood her ground, yanked more feathers loose and acted as though she hadn't a care in the world.

"I see you got supper," he said, pulling up

next to her.

"I did." Another handful of feathers went into the cloth bag. "You get the answers you wanted?"

"I did." He dismounted. "I'll tend to my horse and tell you about it inside."

~~~

Once he had washed up, Uncle Hank rolled the grouse breasts in flour and fried them crisp in bacon grease, while Alice set out biscuits and butter and plates. She was grateful for the lack of alcohol on her uncle's breath as he sat across the table from her a short while later. Ma had told her about their father's drunkenness, and she feared her uncle had chosen the same path when she spied him going into the saloon. She held her tongue, though questions filled her head, bit into fried bird tastier than any Ma had ever made.

Then Uncle Hank told her about his conversation with Pressfield. Alice's heart fell. "I haven't got that kind of money," she said. "I'm guessing you don't either."

"You guess right."

"Then I have no choice but to sign the railroad stock over to that snake and be done with it."

Uncle Hank buttered his second biscuit.
~~~

"Those stocks are worth enough to keep this ranch running for a good many years."

"That don't matter, if I can't pay Pa's debt."

"I may have a way to fix that." He chased half the biscuit with a gulp of coffee before explaining himself. "You know anything about the horse race this Saturday?"

Alice's eyes narrowed. "I saw the flier in the mercantile window. You're not thinking of racing that stallion, are you?"

"You got something against my horse?"

"I've got something against losing money we can't afford to lose on a bad bet." She stabbed at the remains of her meal. "Stallions are tricky to race. Unpredictable."

Her uncle smiled around a mouthful of half-chewed food. "That's why I entered your filly, too."

"Too?"

He nodded and swallowed. "Double our odds of winning."

"More like double our odds of losing," Alice grumbled.

"So you don't think your filly can outrun my palomino?"

Alice stopped her stabbing and stared at him. "I know she can."

"Prove it."

~~~

Hank tightened his grip on the saddle horn and glanced over at Alice and her horse running abreast of him. She leaned low over the filly's stretched-out neck, the scowl gone from between her eyes, the horse's mane whipping at her face. She was smiling. Grinning even. Hank saw the young girl she ought to be, carefree and happy. At the risk of spoiling her mood, he dug his heels into the palomino, demanding more speed. He knew the girl would not cotton to him going easy on her. Plus he needed to find out if his hunch held true.

The palomino stallion was mostly quarter horse with a little Mexican stock in the mix, bred for quick starts, fast reflexes, and endurance. When he told the barkeeper he'd outrun anything after him, it was the horse's endurance more than speed that had served him well. The chestnut filly, on the other hand, looked to have Arabian blood in her, with those wide-spaced eyes, arched neck and long legs – a horse bred for speed.

Well, that filly let his stallion get a full length ahead before deciding she didn't care for the view. They raced neck-and-neck for a short distance, then filly and rider left Hank
~~~

and his stallion swallowing their dust. Those girls reached the fence at the north edge of the field a good thirty yards ahead of them, and it was Hank's turn to grin.

"Still think I made a bad bet?" he asked his niece.

The chestnut filly danced sideways, more run left in her, and Alice laughed. "Race ya back."

"I've got something for you first." Hank pulled the wrapped bar of Swiss chocolate from his inside pocket and held it out to her. "I saw it on the list earlier, figured you might have forgot it," he said, though he didn't take her for the forgetful type. He'd ducked into the mercantile before riding out of town, curious to know what her "near enough" meant when asked if she got everything. Mrs. Henderson had been all too quick to fill him in on what his niece purchased, and to suggest surprising her with one of the dresses hanging on a rack next to the shirts. Hank respectfully declined and bought the chocolate bar instead.

Alice's eyes teared up; her hand shook as she took it from him.

Hank swallowed hard, surprised by her reaction. "I didn't mean for it to make you cry."

She swiped at her eyes with her shirt

sleeve. "It ain't like that," she said, staring at the bar.

"Suppose you explain it then, because I'm purely confused."

She did. Between hiccups and wiping her tears away, she told him about the family Christmas and what that one little hunk of chocolate represented. Hank felt full and empty at the same time. Full with knowing that he could give her a happy memory of her family, and empty that he'd never had such a memory of his own. His childhood memories of Christmas were better left buried.

"You don't play fair, gettin' me to blubber so I can't see straight," Alice said.

Hank thought of Saturday and wondered if he had put his niece in a situation he hadn't ought to have. She was only twelve years old, for God's sake. "Chances are, there will be others in the race, full grown men, who won't play fair. Are you up to it?"

She tucked the chocolate bar inside her shirt, straightened her shoulders, and met him with a look that made him pity any man who got in her way. "Ma taught me a thing or two."

Hank nodded. "Then let's race."

Alice and that filly beat him back to the barn.

Chapter 5

The day warmed Hank's shoulders through his worn cotton shirt as he tightened the final screw on the corral gate hinge. He had come across the hinge and screws laid out on a workbench in the barn, a project Joe Calder no doubt intended to get to but was unable to complete. Hank knew he could never fill Calder's shoes, had no notion of even trying, but he knew his way around tools and aimed to put them to good use. He took pleasure in the way one task led to another, the rhythm of it, the sense of accomplishment at getting a thing done.

The cabin door slammed open and footsteps stomped across the porch. Hank looked up to see Nan storm toward him like a dark cloud prepared to release its fury, and he was the target.

"I want a word with you, Mr. Bonet."

He loosened the rope he'd used to hold the gate in place, looped it around his arm, then faced the storm square on, sure enough of what that word concerned. Alice had been talking about nothing else since yesterday. When Nan rode up on the buckskin a few minutes ago, he knew it was just a matter of time before she got the news.

"What are you thinking, entering Alice in a horse race?" she demanded.

The bright pink flowers on her dress were no match for the flush in her cheeks. She stopped an arm's length from him, her back stiff, shoulders squared, unafraid to face him and speak her mind. Hank appreciated that about her. "It might be quicker if you told me what she said, so's I don't repeat what you already know."

"You hope to win enough money between the two of you to pay off Joe Calder's debt."

"That about sums it up."

"She's just a girl."

The twinge of guilt that made last night's sleep restless danced across his conscience. "I'm not comfortable with my decision, but I stand by it. If you've got another way to make a fast twelve-hundred dollars, I'd sure like to hear it. This ranch, that girl, needs those railroad stocks to survive. It was Joe Calder's plan and I mean to make it happen."

"At the risk of Alice getting hurt."

"I'll be there to look after her."

"I've no doubt," Nan conceded, "but you can't be everywhere at once. You'd need eyes in the back of your head."

"I could use somebody watching my back, that's for certain."

Hank saw a spark in her eyes, the set to her chin that dared challenge – much the way a black-haired beauty from years past use to look at him. The memory brought a familiar pang of loss.

"I'll be there," Nan said, "you can count on it. But it will be Alice's back I'm watching."

"Fair enough." Her assurance eased his mind some. He wasn't a man used to trusting people, but he knew he could trust this woman. Just as Joe Calder had. "Why didn't you tell Alice the ranch isn't hers?"

Nan frowned. "It *is* hers."

"Not according to Pressfield."

The determined set to her chin weakened and she looked away. After a moment, she sighed. "I didn't want her to worry. She's lost enough already. I thought..." Another deep sigh. "I don't know what I thought. That maybe I could keep it quiet until Alice came of age, then I'd sign the ranch back over to her and nobody would be the wiser."

Nan gave him a look he could not read. Pleading? Disappointment? She had not counted on him showing up, he knew that much. What he didn't know was how she felt about it. How she felt about him.

"By rights, the ranch is yours," she finally said. "I will sign the deed over to you, if you so wish. But you must give me your word Alice will be taken care of. If any harm comes to her, I will hunt you down myself."

She would, too. He admired her strength and the tenderness she showed for his niece. In that moment, Hank knew if ever a woman could fill the empty spot in his heart, it would be this one. Just as he knew hitching up with him was the last thing either of them needed. People he allowed himself to care about had a way of ending up dead. He thought of the girl's words to him at the family plot, about keeping his distance. Maybe it was true. Being alone was safer for everybody.

"Better the ranch stay in your hands," he told her. "I've learned to make my own way and not get attached to things."

"Does that include people, Mr. Bonet?"

"Especially people," he said, and turned away, angry with himself for wanting more than he deserved. "Good day to you, Mrs. Trevor." He gathered his tools and headed to the barn.

~~~

Alice went looking for her uncle as soon as she heard Nan ride off, fearing the widow had succeeded in changing his mind about letting her race. She found him drawing his knife blade across her pa's leather strop in the barn. It stopped her for a second, seeing him standing there so much like her pa use to when he was polishing the blade of his folding knife. "Brought over from Wales by my father," he'd tell her with a soft smile. He showed her how to keep the three-inch blade razor sharp for skinning, how to swing it open one-handed if needed, how friction and a firm grip held the tang nestled in the wood handle and prevented the blade from closing on the user's fingers. Alice always figured the knife would be passed down to little Joey though – father to son, over generations. Instead, she carried it tucked in her bib pocket.

Curious to see what her uncle wore strapped to his leg, she moved up beside him.
~~~

The wood handle fit his grip like it had spent a good many years there. Something was carved into the end, but she couldn't make it out. The narrow blade was as long as a man's fingers spread out from pinky to thumb. "Is that a Bowie?" she asked.

"Yes. My father gave it to me when I was eight years old."

It was the first mention he'd made of his folks. "What was he like? Your father."

Uncle Hank continued to draw the blade over the strop in slow, careful strokes, his mouth shut tight.

"Ma wouldn't talk about him either," Alice said, making no attempt to disguise her annoyance, "like he was some kinda ghost."

"Not a ghost. A drunk."

"I already know that much. Ma never said why he drank, just that he was angry all the time."

"Annie was very young when our father took to the bottle hard. Mother said he use to be a fur trapper, beaver mostly, but the demand for pelts played out about the time I was born. He worked as a wagon train scout for a while but hated it. He turned his hate to the bottle, then to his family."

"Is he still alive?"

"I don't know."

"Aren't you curious?"

"No."

The finality in his reply silenced Alice. She turned and began to walk away.

"Alice?"

She stopped and looked back at her uncle. He had sheathed his knife.

"You didn't come out here to talk about my father."

"Are you gonna let me race Saturday?"

"Nothing's changed."

"It's a good plan," she said, on the chance he needed reminding.

He nodded, leaned against the workbench and folded his arms across his chest. "The track will be a half-mile straightaway, from a standing start, down the middle of town. My horse has done his share of cutting, so he's used to getting out quick. You let that filly take her time. Let the others get ahead a bit so you don't get boxed in, then you let her know she's in a race."

Alice had heard him tell her as much already, but she listened again, as though hearing it for the first time. She would listen to his instructions as many times as it took for the chance to race, to settle her debt, and to put

Pressfield in his place.

"I'll remember," she told her uncle.

~~~

Alice was six years old when she saw her first race in Baker City. She remembered her excitement at watching the high-strung horses and their serious-looking riders from the safety of Pa's shoulders. She remembered groups of men arguing and passing money between them, and ladies standing in the shade of the boardwalks, carrying on their own conversations like they hadn't seen each other in too long. Folks scattered about on both sides of the track roped off down the middle of Main Street. More folks than Alice had ever seen in one place.

Today was no different, but for Pa's absence and the way her breakfast sat uneasy on her stomach. Judging by how some of those folks stared at her and her uncle, Alice figured they were being sized up, guessing their odds. She didn't think she wanted to know the odds, for fear her breakfast decided not to stay where it belonged.

Penny's skin quivered and her ears flicked at the unfamiliar noises. Alice patted the filly's neck and tried to convey a calm she did not herself feel. Nan and Jacob followed behind.
~~~

Alice didn't much care for Jacob and his smart-aleck ways, always treating her like she didn't have enough sense to fill a thimble because he was two years older. He probably came along just so he could whoop when she lost. Well, she wouldn't give him the pleasure.

A tall gentleman wearing a gray vest and matching bowler approached them. Uncle Hank reined in and gave a nod. "Hatcher."

The man tipped the brim of his bowler. "Bonet. Six horses are entered, including you and your niece. The race begins at ten."

"All right."

Hatcher looked over at her. "You sure you're ready for this, young lady? Some of those men may not care that you're a girl if you get in their way."

"I don't scare easy, sir."

He smiled. "Your uncle said that about you." Hatcher looked back at Uncle Hank. "Right now the betting is eight to one against the girl. I've got my money on that palomino of yours. Best of luck to both of you." He tipped his hat again and walked away.

Nan rode up alongside. Alice thought she looked especially pretty in her white bodice and dark blue skirt this morning, her golden hair pulled back in a thick braid. "I can tell by the look on your face there's no point in trying to talk you out of doing this," Nan said. "You heed your uncle's advice and you'll do fine."

"Yes, ma'am."

"Jacob and I will be at the other end, near the finish line."

Jacob rode up beside his ma. Like always, his wild, curly hair hung in his face and he had a know-it-all grin. "Yeah," he said, "don't keep us waiting."

Alice narrowed her eyes at him. "You just be sure to stay out of my way."

~~~

Six horses lined up at the north end of Main Street. Two of them had Alice and her filly boxed between them. Hank sized up their riders, men used to spending time in the saddle and accustomed to hard living, by appearances. Something about them didn't set right.

Hank settled his palomino alongside the one on the left. "Fine morning for an honest race," he commented loud enough to be heard some distance. "Be a shame if anybody tried to dirty it up."

The rider gave him a defiant stare. "Look who's callin' who dirty."

Hank had heard such talk too many times
~~~

to let it rankle him. "That's right," he said. "You'd do well to keep your eye on this dirty injun, and leave the girl alone."

"As long as she stays behind me, we ain't got a problem."

"And if she doesn't?"

"We'll see how smart she is, entering a man's race."

Hank's jaw tightened. "If that's the way you want to play it."

"That's the way I'm playin' it."

Hank looked past the rider to Alice staring down the street as if concentrating on the finish line. She'll be all right, he told himself, as long as she remembers what I said.

The starting pistol fired.

~~~

At the sound of the pistol, Penny skittered backwards while the other five horses burst forward. Alice fought to steady the filly and get her pointed in the right direction. Then she saw what her uncle had warned her of as the horses to the right and left of her crashed into each other hard enough to throw them off stride. If Penny hadn't shied, she'd have been crushed between them.

Of all the low-down, dirty tricks! It made Alice mad. Real mad. She went to dig her heels
~~~

into the filly and get in the race, but Uncle Hank cut in front of her. He and the palomino commenced to crowd the tangled horses, giving them a dose of their own medicine. That palomino was bigger than those other two and nearly pushed them clean off the track and onto the boardwalk. Women shrieked and scrambled out of the way.

Seeing her chance, Alice leaned low over Penny's neck and shouted, "Come on, girl!"

Penny lunged into a run, leaving the three horses and their riders to work it out amongst themselves. Alice set her sights on the remaining two horses, now half a dozen lengths ahead. Dust filled the air; she squinted to see through the grit in her eyes, pulled her neckerchief up over her nose and dug her heals into Penny's sides. Penny stretched out and narrowed the distance on the nearest horse's haunches. Its rider attempted to block them, but Penny cut around the opposite side, neat as you please.

"Good girl!"

One more horse, a strawberry roan, to pass. Alice gave Penny free rein. The filly knew what needed doing and had the heart to get it done without her rider's say so. As they closed in on the roan and its rider, Alice realized it was the cowboy from the mercantile. He tossed her a surprised glance then a wink, as she and Penny pulled ahead and left them with a view of their backsides.

Alice believed the race won. She saw the crowd waiting at the finish line. She relaxed in the saddle, but Penny was not having it. Her neck stretched lower and Alice felt the filly's muscles strain for more speed. Then Alice saw the palomino closing in on them from the corner of her eye and realized her uncle had no intention of letting her win the race that easy. She leaned into Penny's neck, making herself as small as possible, shouted, "We're almost there, girl!"

And then they were, crossing the finish line a full length ahead of Uncle Hank and the stallion. People cheered and clapped; a few stomped the dirt in disgust over losing a bet. Jacob whooped and tossed his hat in the air. Alice dismounted and Nan threw her arms around her. Uncle Hank dismounted and started toward them, a big grin on his dusty face.

The last horse to finish was one of the two that had tried to crush her. Alice saw its rider jump off and rush Uncle Hank.

~~~
~~~

Nan screamed. Hank whipped to his left, ducking as he turned. The right hook intended for his face found empty air. Hank came up and jabbed the man hard in the stomach, just below the sternum. It was one of the riders who had tried to hurt Alice, Hank saw, as he brought his other fist down hard on the back of the man's neck, driving him into the dirt. Hank grabbed the knot of the man's neckerchief and twisted, cutting off his air.

"I warned you to play it clean," Hank said.

The man struggled to breathe and Hank tightened his hold.

Alice came up alongside. "Don't kill him just yet."

Why not?

Then shame that he'd been about to kill a man in front of his niece and all the folks gathered around to watch made Hank release his hold. The man gasped and attempted to get to his hands and knees. Alice stepped up and kicked him hard enough in the ribs that she nearly threw herself off balance. It had to have cracked bone, Hank thought. The man grunted and collapsed.

"Now you can kill him, if you want," the girl said, and walked away.

The man curled in pain at Hank's feet

didn't appear interested in continuing the fight. Hank wasn't either. "I think he's learned his lesson." He looked to the other rider keeping his distance at the edge of the crowd. "Who put you up to this?"

"I don't know what you're talking about." But even from this distance, Hank saw the guilt and fear in the man's eyes.

"You didn't enter the race to win," Hank said. "You entered it to make sure the girl *didn't*. Who paid you?" He took a step closer and the man jumped, ready to bolt. It didn't matter. Hank already had his suspicions. "Run on back to your boss and tell him that any man who picks on my niece answers to me. Now collect your partner and get out of my sight."

Hank turned and saw Nan coming toward him. He couldn't tell if she was ready to strike him or kiss him. He surely wouldn't have minded the latter, but she did neither.

"I warned you there could be trouble," she said.

"And I dealt with it."

Nan gave a half smile. "With Alice's help."

"Yes." Hank wondered how many classroom boys went home with broken ribs before his niece was told not to come back to school. His sister had taught the girl well.

"Thank you," he said to Nan.

"For what?"

"Watching my back."

Her lips parted as if to argue the point, but somewhere in the few seconds Hank and she stood looking at each other, she seemed to change her mind. "You're welcome."

Hank turned to Alice. "I'm going to collect our winnings from Hatcher," he told her. "Then we're paying a visit to Pressfield. Be ready."

Chapter 6

Nan and Jacob took the horses to the livery for a rubdown and grain. Alice matched her uncle's long strides as they made their way to the bank. The pocket of his leather vest bulged with more money than she'd ever seen in one place.

"You think Pressfield paid those men to take me out of the race, don't you?" she asked.

"He's the one had the most to gain by it."

"Then you should have let me bring my rifle, so I can put him in the ground with the rest of the snakes."

Uncle Hank stopped and stared down at her. "Have you ever shot a man?"

"I've shot – " *gopher, rabbit, deer. But a man?* Alice swallowed. "No."

"Pulling the trigger's easy. It's the living

with it after that's hard."

"Have *you* ever shot a man?"

"This isn't about me," he said and continued walking.

Alice stayed put. "You didn't answer my question."

Uncle Hank turned, and she saw the bitterness in his face. "There are those who challenged a half-breed's right to live in a white man's world. It did not always end well for them."

Alice remembered the times Ma had been shunned for her Arapaho blood, how it hurt her. How angry it made her. Her brother carried that same hurt and anger. It showed in his eyes, the tightness in his voice, as if saying it didn't come easy. Alice remembered her ma's words, *Never take a life without good reason.*

"I reckon you did what you needed to survive," she told Uncle Hank. "I reckon I can survive fine with Pressfield getting old and gray in his fancy bank." She marched past him. "Let's get this done."

~~~

Pressfield didn't look as surprised to see them as Hank half expected. Either news traveled fast, or he had watched the end of the race from his office window and saw the
~~~

outcome for himself.

"We've come to settle Joseph Calder's business," Hank told him.

"Of course." Pressfield pushed a sheet of paper already laid out on his desk toward them. "This is the current balance due."

Hank glanced at the sum. It had grown, but not beyond the interest rate he'd been quoted. He pulled the roll of bills from his pocket and began counting, while Alice stood quiet at his side. He put the money on the paper and slid it back across the desk.

Pressfield took care to do a recount, then signed the paper and extended it to Hank. "Your receipt."

"It belongs to Alice Calder," Hank said.

Pressfield gave a tight-lipped nod and handed the paper to Alice. She made to fold it away. "Read it first," Hank told her.

"It's a simple receipt of payment," Pressfield said with the impatience of a man speaking to the ignorant.

Alice glared at him, took a seat, and began reading. She took her time. Hank knew her to be a fast reader and suspected her of deliberately testing the bank president's patience. If Pressfield suspected the same, he could do nothing about it. The desk clock ticked each slow second.

Finally the girl stood and folded the paper in quarters. "It's as he says." She tucked the receipt into the back pocket of her bibbed overalls.

"Now the stocks," Hank said.

More papers slid across the desk, a thick stack this time. Without being told, Alice sat and commenced looking them over. After a few minutes, she nodded at Hank and tucked the stocks behind her bib.

"That concludes our business," Pressfield stated. He pushed up out of his deep chair and reached for the gray frock coat hanging off to his side. "Now, if you'll excuse me – "

"There is one more thing." Hank moved around the desk so it was no longer between them. Alice backed up to the door and leaned against it. They had Pressfield boxed in, and he knew it.

"Now see here," he blustered. "Mr. Calder's business is settled and – "

"Mine isn't."

"Yours?" The banker stepped back, bumped the corner of the desk with his hip, eyed Alice standing at the door as if weighing his chances.

Alice had that look on her face Hank had

come to recognize, the one that dared any man to cross her.

Pressfield looked back at Hank. "I assure you, we have – "

"Only a coward pays somebody else to do his dirty work."

"I have no idea what you're talking about."

"People say injuns have a keen sense of smell." Hank flared his nostrils. "For instance, I can smell when a man is lying to me."

Sweat ran from Pressfield's thinning hairline and into his smartly trimmed beard. "I assure you, no one has been paid to do whatever you deem me guilty of."

"Now you speak the truth." Hank figured the two men who had gone after Alice were sitting in a saloon by now, washing the bad taste out of their mouths. With any luck, they were letting those around them know the source of that taste. "Before this day ends," he told Pressfield, "I intend to see the entire town hears of what you did. And if you or anyone else under your hire threatens my niece again, or steps onto Calder property, it won't be the girl doing the shooting."

His piece said, Hank did not wait for a response from Pressfield. He and Alice left the man standing in his own sour sweat.

~~~

Alice drew in a deep breath once she and her uncle stepped out of the bank, grateful for the smell of dust and manure. She had done snakes wrong, comparing them to Pressfield. Snakes didn't stink that way. The restaurant next door was serving folks midday meal: boiled potatoes, steaks, fresh coffee. Her queasy stomach settled to a low grumble for food.

"Did you mean what you said in there?" she asked her uncle. "About being able to smell a lie?"

"Doesn't take a good nose to tell when a man's lying. You can see it in his eyes and by the way he stands."

"And how much he sweats." Alice shuddered and her uncle smiled.

"Yes." His smile faded and his eyes got serious. "I'm not proud of the way I talked back there. Don't let me catch you using that word. I only use it to throw a person off balance."

Alice did not need to ask him which word he meant. She'd heard it often enough from others to know it for the disrespect it was intended. "How do you plan to let people know what Pressfield did?"

"If what he says is true and he didn't pay
~~~

those men, it won't be long before their tongues loosen. And I said as much to Hatcher when I collected our money. I s'pect he'll talk it around. You know this town better than I do. What's the best way to let folks know about a thing, outside of the local watering hole?"

Alice didn't need to think long on her answer. "Mrs. Henderson at the mercantile."

~~~

That evening, Alice sat on the porch rail, watching the sun fade behind the mountains and thinking on the day's events. Her debt was paid, and she'd recovered the railroad stocks. It was a comfortable feeling, knowing the ranch was on solid ground, thanks to her pa's planning ahead and her uncle's grit.

Once Mrs. Henderson had been assured that Alice was unharmed, her eyes shined at the prospect of telling folks about Pressfield's crooked doings. "I never did trust that man," the woman declared.

People Alice didn't know had stopped to congratulate her on winning the race; one fellow admitted to having bet against her but held no hard feelings, on account she was a girl and he'd never seen the like. "If that's the kind of stock you're raising," he said, "I'll come by in the spring. Could use me a good saddle horse."
~~~

"I've got three already broke to saddle," Alice told him. "No need to wait."

He gave a hearty laugh. "I lose my money to you in a race and now you want to sell me a horse. I like you, girl. I just may take you up on your offer."

Alice had not considered the possibility that her winning the race might benefit horse sales. That was a good feeling too. The two- and three-year-olds could start being trained to saddle next year. And there were the new foals; they'd need to get used to being handled and learn to accept a rope harness. The bay's foal would be the last of the season.

Alice's gaze slid to the paddock. The bay mare paced a restless circle in the fading daylight. After a moment, she stopped and laid down. An instant later she was up again, her tail extended. Even at this distance, Alice could see the amniotic sac beginning to emerge. She leaped to her feet and raced to the barn.

Uncle Hank had kicked his boots off and was stretched out on top of his bed covers, reading the book of Wordsworth poems she'd lent him.

"The bay's ready to drop her foal," Alice said, unable to contain the excitement in her voice. No matter how many times she'd witnessed it, the wonder of birth always had that effect on her.

Uncle Hank smiled and set the book aside. "It's about time." He shoved his stockinged feet into his boots and trailed her to the paddock with the lantern.

The mare was down again, on her side and straining. Inside the amniotic sac a small hoof protruded, soon followed by another.

"That's a welcome sight," Uncle Hank said.

"She's always been one of Pa's favorites," Alice told him. "Never puts up a fuss, just gets down to business. She's a good mother, too."

There was little for Alice and her uncle to do but encourage the mare during the hardest part of the process: pushing the foal's shoulders through. Alice pulled the sac away from the foal's head as the rest of its body slid out. A handsome colt. The bay lie exhausted for a few minutes, then sat up and began cleaning him. Within an hour, the colt was standing, nursing, and pooping.

It was just about the best way to finish off an already exciting day, Alice decided.

~~~

One day eased its way into the next. Daylight grew scarcer, evenings cooler. Hank carried an extra blanket out to his cot in the
~~~

barn and kept a fire burning longer in the potbelly stove.

After Mrs. Henderson ran out of customers to gossip to about Pressfield's shameful behavior, the bank remained standing, and Pressfield continued to sit in his office overlooking Main Street. Folks had banking to tend to, after all, and it didn't make sense to travel miles out of their way to do it. That took precious time from running businesses and tending to chores and family responsibilities, though Mrs. Henderson let it be known that a few people chose to keep their money at home now, rather than have anything to do with the bank's president. Word got around that interest rates had dropped a bit on loans. Incentive to draw in business, Hank figured. All things considered, it was the most he and Alice could hope for.

And the fellow who told Alice he was in need of a good saddle horse stopped in and bought the three-year-old sorrel gelding.

Life settled into a comfortable routine. Alice agreed to let Hank do much of the cooking, outside of baking biscuits. She said kneading bread dough helped her think. That suited Hank fine. He could say the same about cooking up a pot of stew or frying a batch of eggs and bacon. Time spent helping an ailing trail cook taught him how to put together a meal with what was on hand and have it served up in a hurry.

Mares led their foals around the pasture, teaching them to graze and become more independent. Soon they'd be weaned and exploring the boundaries of the ranch on their own. Pasture grass was abundant, and Joe Calder had stored enough hay in preparation for winter that Hank could turn his mind to other matters.

He came across a break in the north fence and strung new barbed wire, then Alice rode with him to round up a couple strays in the canyon. Together, he and his niece moved the horses to the south pasture to prevent overgrazing. The girl's way with horses continued to surprise and please him. She could handle her own at the end of a crosscut saw, too, said she helped her pa cut wood many a time. And once Hank had a pile of firewood split, she helped with stacking. Come time to do the washing, Alice got down the tubs and washboard, Hank packed hot water from the cabin, and between them they scrubbed, rinsed, and hung long underwear, britches, shirts and neckerchiefs to dry. They canned pickles and tomatoes and green beans from the garden, and put up wild blackberry preserves. When a thing needed done, they shared the chores as equals.

In the evenings, they read. With Alice's tutoring, Hank made his way through Shakespeare's *King Lear* and learned how Cordelia, the king's youngest and most cherished daughter, came to be banished from the kingdom.

Hank could understand his niece's attraction to Cordelia's unwillingness to lie to the father she loved so dear. "But I don't understand what that has to do with a milk cow," he said.

Alice shrugged. "Nothing. I just liked the sound of it."

"And your horse Penny?"

"Short for Penelope, the wife of Odysseus."

"The fellow who sacrificed six of his men to a cliff monster."

"She stayed faithful to him, even though he was gone for years. I like the idea of a horse staying true. Your palomino got a name?"

"Never gave it much thought." To be honest, the palomino was the first animal he'd ever owned long enough to grow an attachment to.

"An animal stays with you long, does right by you, he deserves a name."

"What do you suggest?"

"It ain't my place. He's your horse."

"I'll think on it."

Hank considered *The Last of the Mohicans* too sad a tale to claim enjoyment of, found Wordsworth's poem "I Wandered Lonely as a Cloud" more to his liking. The idea of a simple field of flowers easing a man's pensive mood appealed to him. Many a time he'd sat atop his horse and marveled at the beauty of his surroundings, be it the sun turning a band of hills the color of gold in Wyoming, or a summer rain sweeping across the Chihuahuan Desert.

Nan Trevor continued to ride over often with butter or milk, and on rare occasions half a pie she'd rescued from her sons before they had a chance to devour it. From time to time she'd help Alice with sewing, the one skill Alice seemed to be all thumbs at. Hank enjoyed the widow's presence, her gentle ways, the pleasing sound of her laughter. He did not take her being there lightly, for she and her boys had their hands full tending to their own ranch and small stock of horses and hogs. Jacob and William were hard workers, but they were only fourteen and ten and sometimes needed a stronger back or pair of hands.

Alice told him that after Mr. Trevor died, her pa went over to do what he could to help out. Joe Calder's death had left both families shorthanded. Hank assisted the trimming of a cantankerous mare's hoof, put a wheel back on their wagon, replaced a hay shed post. He was glad to help, took pleasure in the time spent with Nan and her boys.

But he knew the day was coming, and soon, when he and Alice needed to consider hiring a ranch hand to take up the slack.

Chapter 7

Frost glistened on the trees bordering the pasture. The grass crunched beneath the horses' hooves as they grazed. Alice and her uncle chipped a thin sheen of ice from the water trough, fed the chickens, and were sitting down to the morning meal when they heard someone ride up.

"Too early to be Nan," Alice said, and went to the door. There stood the cowboy from the mercantile, bundled in a woolen coat. Alice's cheeks warmed in spite of the crisp outdoor air.

"Pardon the intrusion, ma'am." He removed his hat. "Is your uncle around?"

Uncle Hank stepped up behind her. "I'm Henry Bonet. What can I do for you?"

"I thought you should know there's a

handful of men in town asking about a half-breed riding a palomino."

Alice felt the air around her uncle go still, like the quiet that comes upon a wild animal being stalked. "Step inside and warm yourself," he said.

The cowboy came in, hung his coat on a peg by the door and rested his hat over it. Alice went to the stove to pour another cup of coffee, careful not to slop.

"Thank you," he said, and wrapped his hands around the cup to warm them. "You still riding that fine filly?"

"Penny," Alice said with a self-conscience smile. "Every chance I get."

"Have a seat," Uncle Hank offered. "Fix you a plate?"

"It sure smells good. Don't mind if I do." He pulled up a chair and sat. "Name's Pete Christian."

"Sally's brother," Alice said, surprised she hadn't seen the resemblance until now. She handed him a plate of biscuits and gravy with thick slices of bacon on the side.

He nodded his thanks. "You knew my sister?"

Alice sat across the table from him. "She stuck up for me in school."

Pete smiled. "That was Sally's way." His smile faded. "Smallpox took her about the same time your family passed."

"I didn't know. I'm sorry."

"It broke Ma's heart. She claimed she couldn't live in a country that would take her girl from her. She and Pa sold the place and went back east to live with kin."

"But you chose to stay," Uncle Hank commented.

Pete's cheeks brightened and he looked down at his plate. "I got me a girl I'm kinda sweet on in town."

Alice would be a liar if she said his words didn't cause a jealous pang. But she got over it quick enough when he declared, "These are some mighty fine biscuits."

"What do you do for work?" Uncle Hank asked.

"Been drifting, picking up jobs here and there. Just got off a trail ride in Idaho."

Alice caught her uncle looking over at her and could see what he was thinking. It was something they'd been talking about. She appreciated him giving her a say, and it would be nice to help out the brother of a girl who had shown her kindness. She nodded her consent.

"You're welcome to stick around and help out here," he told Pete. "The pay's fair, three meals a day, and you can bunk in the barn if you need a place to lay your head."

"I'd like that. Thank you, sir."

"Call me Hank." They shook on it.

Though nothing was said, Alice knew it was time to let her uncle move into Ma and Pa's room. The thought of someone else sleeping in her folks' bed made their passing all the more real, but the room had been sitting empty for nigh on four months. Uncle Hank was family, now more than ever.

Pete was on his second round of biscuits and gravy when Uncle Hank asked, "These men you saw in town anybody you know?"

Pete shook his head. "They didn't look the type to be real friendly, neither."

"How many are there?"

"Five, near as I saw. One of 'em has a long scar on his face." Pete traced a line from the corner of his eye to his jawbone. "He gave the orders."

Uncle Hank got a hard look in his eyes that scared Alice. "Do you know him?" she asked.

"He's my father's younger brother, Nathan Bonet."

Stunned, Alice said, "How come you never

let on you had an uncle? How come Ma never talked about him?"

"Nathan Bonet isn't the kind of man you want to know." Uncle Hank turned to Pete. "Did he say what he wanted with me?"

"Just that it was private family business."

"Maybe he's got news about your father," Alice offered.

"If he does, you can bet it isn't good." Uncle Hank looked to Pete again. "Has anybody told him I'm here?"

"Not to my knowing. I was in the mercantile when they came in for supplies. The Hendersons didn't let on they knew where you were. The man you call Nathan didn't look like he believed them, but he paid for his goods and left. I made sure I wasn't being watched before I rode over."

"It's not going to take him long to figure it out."

"You think he'll come here?" Alice asked. Her uncle's reaction to Pete's news had her purely confused.

"Not if I can help it." Uncle Hank stood, told Pete, "After you finish eating, meet me in the barn. I'll show you where to bunk and get you squared away."

~~~
~~~

Hank saddled the palomino, strapped the saddlebags in place. People were lying for him, and those lies could get them hurt. Worse, Nathan and his men might show up at the ranch. Hank wasn't about to let that happen. He had no idea what Nathan wanted with him. He intended to find out, but first he needed to make sure the people he cared for were safe. He just hoped he didn't run out of time.

He took a liking to Pete Christian right off. Not just for stepping in to warn him, but for choosing to make his own way in life. Like Alice, Pete had grown up in this area, so when he entered the barn a few minutes later, Hank asked, "If a man was to set a trap, where would that place be?"

Pete nodded east. "The mountains'd be your best bet. Lots of places to hole up, places that aren't easy to get to."

"I could use your help, if you've a mind."

"Name it."

"Once I find what I'm looking for, I need those men to follow me, without letting them close enough to get off a decent shot. Meet me at the edge of town midafternoon. Let me know where they're at, then give a shout that you saw me and point them in my direction."

"I'll be there."

"Don't tell Alice what we've talked about,"
Hank said. "If I don't come back, it's because
I'm dead. I know it's a lot to ask, the two of us
having just met and all, but look after the girl?"

"Like she was my little sister."

~~~

Alice heard Pete ride off and looked out
the kitchen window. Her uncle was in the
corral, tying his bedroll to the palomino. Her
stomach constricted, and she went to confront
him. "What're you fixin' to do?"

"What I can to keep those men away from
you and this ranch."

"But you don't even know what they want.
Aren't you curious? We should at least go talk
—"

Her uncle rounded on her. "You don't *talk*
with Nathan Bonet."

Alice flinched at the harshness in his voice.
"But he's your uncle."

"By blood only." He turned away, gathered
two boxes of cartridges and put one in each
saddlebag, cinched the flaps. "If he steps foot
on your land, shoot him. You'll know him by
the scar on his face. Don't try to talk to him,
just shoot him dead."

A chill ran through Alice. "What did he
do?"
~~~

"I wish there was time to explain." Uncle Hank looked her in the eyes when he said it, and she knew it for the truth. "But every minute we stand here talking about him, he and his men are getting closer."

"I'm going with you then."

"Like hell you are."

Alice refused to show how his words stung. He'd never spoken cross to her before. She straightened her shoulders. "You need somebody watchin' your back."

He hesitated, and for a brief moment Alice took hope she had changed his mind. Then he gathered the reins and swung into the saddle. "This is something I've got to do on my own. I'm liable to make mistakes if you're along to worry about, and any mistake with this bunch could mean the end of it, for me and for you."

Fear climbed up Alice's spine, tied a knot of apprehension in her stomach. "Where will you go?"

"It's better I don't say."

"But – "

"I'm not going to argue about it, Alice. You stay put, and you stay safe. Don't open the door to anybody you don't know. And keep that Winchester by your side, you hear me?"

"I hear you. But if you're not back in a

couple days, I'll come looking for you."

"You'll do no such thing. Pete will be back before dark. With his help, and Nan and her boys close by, you go on best you can. Make a good life for yourself."

Alice's breath caught and tears blurred her eyes, no matter how hard she tried to hold them off. "You don't plan on comin' back, do you?"

He gave a long, drawn-out breath. "I didn't plan on any of this," he said soft-like. "It's just the way things are. If I'm able to, by God I will. But not before I've gotten the answers I need."

"Promise?"

He looked at her long and hard. "I promise."

Alice swiped the tears from her face, set her chin, and said, "You're gonna need grub."

~~~

It wasn't Hank's habit to make promises. Putting distance between him and the ranch, his saddlebags packed with more food than he'd be able to eat in a month, he hoped to hell he could keep this one. A yearning to glance back at the place he'd come to call home dug deep, but he kept his eyes trained on the road in front of him and away from the look of abandonment on Alice's face.
~~~

Regret pressed like a fist in his chest. He should have told her right off what kind of blood she came from. His father, Thomas Bonet, had been a pathetic, broken man who turned mean when drunk, but his younger brother was born mean. Nathan Bonet didn't need drink or cause to draw down on a man. Hank had seen him beat a man to death, then continue to beat on the man's lifeless body until somebody pulled him off. It did not come as a surprise that Annie kept it from the girl.

The day Nathan struck Hank's mother, Hank – all but seven years old – grabbed up a skinning knife and drove the blade into the man's forearm. Nathan yanked it out and swung it at Hank's throat. Thomas Bonet had not yet made it to the bottom of his daily bottle, was still sober enough to slash his brother's face and throw him out.

"No man touches my squaw and brats but me!" he raged. Then he rounded on Hank. "Boy, if you're gonna pull a knife on a man, you damn well better learn to do it right."

Thomas Bonet had traveled far as a trapper, had learned his way around a blade from a man who crafted them by trade. Over time, he earned a reputation for being better with a knife than a gun. In his sober moments, he began teaching Hank what he remembered, gave him one of his prized Bowies to practice with. Hank carved his initials in the handle, then endured his father's wrath over defacing a finely crafted tool. It mattered not to Hank. Once marked, the Bowie became his to keep.

Nathan Bonet, scarred for life by his own brother, became someone to avoid at all costs. And now he was in Baker City, hunting. There was no other way to look at it, to Hank's way of thinking. Nathan was hunting him.

Hank's thoughts went to Nan. If Nathan took a notion to question folks at neighboring ranches, she and her boys were at risk too. Nan had watched his back; now it was on him to repay the debt. Though she persisted upon addressing him as Mr. Bonet, he wanted to believe she had feelings for him, as he did for her. He would miss her. But she was a strong woman and she'd do well, with or without him. He relied on Pete to be there if she needed help.

The mountains. It was already late September. Snow would fall soon. He needed to find a place to hole up, a defensive spot with a good lookout. A place where he could turn things to his advantage.

With the ranch behind him, Hank and the

palomino snaked along a trail up through the pines. Fingers of sunlight stretched between needled branches, melting the morning frost. Sparrows chirped and trilled to each other. Under better circumstances, he would have found cause to linger and appreciate the fine clear morning, breathe deep the fragrance of evergreens, sap, and damp earth.

Resentment grew in him as he rode. A man ought to have a right to live the life of his choosing. Four months ago, he would not have been able to say what sort of life he wanted. Drifting had suited him fine. That changed when he met his niece. Having someone need him, care whether he came or went, changed him. He felt an unfamiliar wholeness, foreign, yet to his liking.

No one would take that from him. Especially not Nathan Bonet.

~~~

Alice stood at the porch railing and continued to watch the road long after her uncle was out of sight. A quarter of a mile, Pa said. She had taken his word for it, just as she took her uncle's word that he'd return if able. He left her no choice.

For a few short months, she had felt part of a family again, and now she stood alone.
~~~

Possibly for good this time.

He would go to the mountains, she figured. There were caves and draws where a person could stay hid, become the hunter instead of the hunted. She and her ma use to forage hawthorn and yarrow root, huckleberries and mushrooms in the woods and foothills. Alice knew every trail by heart, knew the best places to duck for shelter in a sudden spring downpour.

Her uncle was a stranger to those things, and the mountains were not kind to the careless. Late last fall a man hunting elk stumbled upon the body of a fifteen-year-old boy gone missing over a year before. He had tumbled a hundred feet from a steep, narrow trail. Folks said the boy likely didn't see the drop-off until it was too late. Alice knew her uncle to be a careful man, but he didn't know the area the way she did.

There had to be something she could do, but what? Outside of a scar on his face, she didn't know what Nathan Bonet looked like, could walk right into him unawares. Uncle Hank was right. She could end up doing more harm than good.

It was no fault of hers she didn't know anything about the man. And the one person who could give her answers just rode off. She wanted to hate Uncle Hank for not being truthful with her, but she'd settle for seeing him again so she could give him a piece of her mind.

A horse whinnied, pulling her from her thoughts. Nan rode up wearing a pretty blue dress and a bright smile. Alice burst into tears.

"What is it, child? Has something happened to Henry?" Nan dismounted and hurried up the steps to pull Alice into her arms. She smelled of rose water.

Embarrassment over her tears did not prevent Alice from catching Nan's use of her uncle's formal first name. Alice had suspected, had seen the way the widow looked at him when she thought no one watched. "Uncle Hank is fine," she said, "for now."

Nan pulled back to look her in the eyes. "He's in trouble though, isn't he?"

Alice nodded.

"Let's go inside." Nan guided her toward the door.

Alice rinsed her face at the wash basin, then poured two coffees and took them to the table. She told Nan about Pete and who the men looking for Uncle Hank were and about his promise.

"I'm sure your uncle is doing what he thinks is right," Nan said, though she didn't do a very good job of hiding the worry in her voice.

"There's got to be a way to help. I could follow him while – "

"No!" Nan set her cup down hard, slopping coffee on the table. "You will do as he said and stay put. You're safer here."

Alice was getting mighty tired of everybody telling her what to do, but she chose not to trouble Nan with her thoughts. The widow had concerns of her own aplenty without her adding to them. She mopped up the spilled coffee with a dish towel, then asked, "Did Ma say anything to you about her uncle?"

"There was never any mention of an uncle. She spoke mostly of her mother and how much she missed her."

"Ma said Grandma Ela was a quiet person, and smart. Not white-man smart, she couldn't read or write, but she taught Ma many of the Arapaho ways, and Ma passed them on to me."

"Yes. It was important to your mother that you know your heritage. She spoke often of her brother, also."

Alice looked down at her coffee, ashamed of how she used to get angry whenever her ma's brother was mentioned. "I remember hating him," she admitted, "a man I never met, because Ma always looked so sad when she talked about him."

"But now?"

Saying she loved somebody didn't come easy for Alice. Her family had been better at showing their love than saying the words. How did she feel about Uncle Hank?

"If he gets himself killed," she told Nan, "I'll never forgive him."

Chapter 8

The sun had nearly reached its peak when Hank found what he was looking for. He had stopped for a midday meal in a grassy clearing with a trickle of a stream running through it, helped himself to the biscuits and cold bacon Alice packed. He discovered the book of Wordsworth's poetry tucked deep in the saddlebag and smiled. As he considered the wisdom of taking a few minutes to lose himself in the poet's words, the call of a crow drew his attention to the far edge of the clearing.

That's where he spied a cut in the hillside. He left his horse to graze and drink while he checked it out. A slim path, just wide enough for a horse and rider, carved into the side of the hill and led to a narrow ledge at the mouth of a cave halfway up the slope. Inaccessible from above, it had a clean line of sight over the trees. Anyone approaching by that route could be spotted long before reaching the entrance.

The cave went back a few feet, then took a natural curve and opened into an area large enough for a man and horse to set up a neat camp out of view. Other than a few squirrel and raccoon tracks, the cave had not been used in some time, the remains of a fire, long cold and scattered, in the corner. A meager pile of firewood sat nearby. The smell of damp earth hung in the confined space.

Hank left the cave. While the palomino continued to graze, he retraced the route they had taken to the clearing on foot. He gazed up the hillside often for signs of the cave from below. Trees and scrub concealed both the entrance and the cut leading to it.

Satisfied, Hank returned to the clearing, led his horse to the cave and unloaded the saddlebags and bedroll. Climbing into the saddle, he gave the palomino its head, allowing it to choose its footing on the slim path.

Then they headed for Baker City.

~~~

Pete sat in the shade of a lone cedar tree, whittling. Hank dismounted and moved in close. He saw the kid had a clear view of the
~~~

saloon, but was back far enough so as not to be easily noticed by anybody leaving the establishment.

"Been in there about half an hour now," Pete said, pointing with the piece of wood in his hand. It looked to be a dog or wolf.

"All of them?"

"Yep."

They both knew what needed doing, but Hank was in no hurry. "You're pretty good with that pocketknife."

"Fair. My pa can carve a hunk of wood so it looks like the real thing." He chuckled softly. "One time he carved a big rat, rubbed it down with stove ash to make it look natural, then left it on the floor 'neath the supper table for Ma to find. She liked to bring the house down with her screamin' and swinging her broom at that wooden rat. Once she realized it wasn't real, she lit after Pa with the broom."

Hank smiled. "Sounds like your pa has a risky sense of humor."

"He enjoyed his jokes, had a laugh that sounded like it come up from the soles of his shoes." Pete looked down at the animal figure in his hands. "Then sister Sally died and he stopped laughing. It was like all the joy in him disappeared, buried in the ground along with her coffin."

Hank did not have words to ease the boy's heart. He knew there were none. He placed a hand on his shoulder. "You ready?"

Pete stood, folded his knife and put it in his hip pocket. He stared at the animal he'd carved, as though uncertain what to do with it.

"Mind if I keep that?" Hank asked. At the boy's questioning look, he said, "I could use me a good luck charm."

Pete handed it over and said, "I'll give you to the end of the street before I start shouting."

"You be sure to stand clear," Hank told him.

Pete nodded. "Best of luck to you."

They shook hands and Pete headed down the boardwalk, toward the saloon. Hank mounted up. It was a good plan.

But just as the boy reached the front of the saloon, Nathan Bonet stepped out.

Pete jerked to a stop as though caught off guard. Hank knew no matter what the kid said or did at that point, it wasn't going to wipe the look of suspicion from Nathan Bonet's face. He couldn't hear what Nathan said to the boy, but could guess at Nathan's intentions when his hand moved for his pistol.

Hank gave a loud, piercing whistle that

caused the palomino to sidestep beneath him. "You looking for me?" he shouted.

Nathan drew, turned in Hank's direction searching for a target. Hank was tempted to pull his rifle and end it right there. Pete had flattened himself against the side of the building, making Nathan an easy mark.

But Hank needed answers. He whooped and reined his horse around. A bullet thwacked the trunk of that lone cedar next to him an instant before he heard the gun's report. Seemed his good luck charm was working already. Hank spurred his horse for the hills.

~~~

A fresh batch of biscuits cooled on the table. Alice cleaned the dishes, then took up her rifle to check on the horses. The afternoon had warmed enough to go without a coat, and she squinted against the sharp sun in a clear, fall sky. Nan told her to trust her uncle's judgment, and that's what she intended to do, go on about her business, tend to the ranch, try not to think about all the things that could go wrong with his plan. Whatever that plan may be.

Halfway to the barn, she spotted Pete riding in, a bedroll and saddlebags across the
~~~

back of his strawberry roan. She had a ranch hand now. Pa use to hire extra help from time to time, especially during foaling season. If snowfall was bad this winter, they...*she* would need help haying the horses and keeping fresh water out. She made a note to herself to check Pa's books and see what he use to pay.

For all she knew, Uncle Hank had already settled terms of payment with Pete when they were in the barn and out of her earshot. Which had her wondering what else her uncle may have discussed with the new hand.

"Afternoon," Pete said, reining his horse at the corral gate.

Not one to dance around a subject, Alice asked, "Did Uncle Hank tell you where he was going?"

Pete dismounted before answering. "I can't say."

Maybe because he didn't know, but Alice guessed otherwise. "Keeping me in the dark ain't doing him any favors. What if he gets himself hurt and nobody's around to help?"

"You can help him by not getting yourself hurt." He looked hard at her. "Those men that're after him? They won't care if you get in the way of a bullet."

Frustrated, Alice argued, "I may not be

good at math, but I'm smart enough to figure out two against five is better odds than one all by himself. Three against five is even better, if you was to come with me."

"And who'd take care of the ranch, the horses, while we're off getting shot at?"

"The horses will fair just fine on their own for a few days."

Pete shook his head. "I gave your uncle my word I'd keep you out of harm's way, and that's what I mean to do, whether you like it or not."

Alice stepped in close, daring him. "What're you gonna do to stop me?"

He met her stare for stare, then threw his arms out in exasperation. "Nothin'," he said. "I ain't gonna do nothin'. You're as bullheaded as Sally use to be. If you've a mind to get yourself killed, I won't try to stop you. I'm just the hired hand, at least until there ain't nobody left alive to work for. And if you've changed your mind about that, let me know right now and I'll get back on my horse."

Alice did not want him to leave. And she felt bad about irritating him into considering it. She was being selfish. If she lit out and something happened to her, Pete would blame himself. She didn't need anybody to tell her that he already carried the burden of his sister's death. Same as she carried the weight of Joey's passing. Not a day went by that she didn't ask the Great Spirit why her little brother died instead of her. Being the oldest, Pete surely asked the same question of whoever he prayed to.

"You hungry?" she asked him.

He frowned at her switching subjects on him, then gave a self-conscious grin. "Ma says I must have a hollow leg. I'm always hungry."

"We'll have us a bite to eat, then check on the horses."

~~~

Hank counted on it taking Nathan and his men some minutes to get to the livery and saddle up. He wove his horse through a stand of young firs, avoiding the route he'd traveled earlier. It was slower going, but he didn't want to make it easy for his pursuers by leading them directly to the trailhead. He gambled on them being as unfamiliar with the layout of the land as he had been. Nathan more than likely rounded up his gang in Wyoming, men he knew and trusted – as near as Nathan trusted any man – from close to home. Hank hoped to use that to his advantage.

He skirted a meadow where a handful of elk grazed at the far edge. Above them a red-
~~~

tailed hawk hung nearly motionless on an air current, casting its shadow across the grasses. Wordsworth's poem about daffodils came to Hank's mind, though their season had long passed and only a few faded bellflowers dotted the meadow. Hank wondered at the beauty before him, like a painter might take it in. Then he and the palomino were back in the evergreens and climbing.

They picked up the trail shortly and followed it to the clearing. No sounds came from behind, so Hank allowed his horse to graze and drink, while he gathered another armload of firewood to add to the stockpile in the cave. He kept his eye on the palomino, and when the horse's head came up and his ears twitched, hearing something Hank could not, Hank led him to the cave.

Not long after staking his horse a safe distance from the entrance, Hank heard them too: the snap of hooves on dried branches, a horse's neigh, a muffled curse. He set up with a box of rounds and his rifle to the side of the cave's opening. He could not see the trail below the bank without revealing himself, but he had a clean shot at anyone who attempted to approach the cave by way of that narrow hillside cut.

Hank didn't know what kind of deal Nathan struck with the other men, nor did he care. They'd made their choice. There was only one he needed alive.

Movement pulled Hank from his thoughts. He did not recognize the man cautiously making his way toward the cave, pistol drawn. Hank shouldered his rifle, took aim, and called, "Another step and you're a dead man."

Two hasty shots struck the cave entrance in response; Hank fired. The man grunted and glanced down at the growing blood stain on the front of his shirt. Then his legs gave out and he tumbled over the edge.

"That you, half-breed?" Nathan called from behind cover at the other end of the cut.

"You know it is," Hank shouted.

"You plan to pick us off one by one?"

"Those men with you are free to leave. I'll even let them collect their dead partner on the way out."

"I've got a better idea. Give yourself up and let's talk."

Hank gave a bitter laugh. "I've seen how you talk. You can tell me why you're hunting me from here, or I start looking for more targets."

"We're taking you in for the murder of my

brother," Nathan shouted.

Thomas Bonet was dead? Hank felt nothing at the news. "What makes you think I did it?"

Another man shouted, "We all know it was your knife sticking out of his chest, *Enojado*."

Only one person had ever called him by that name: *Angry One*. "How long's it been, Mateo?"

"Half a lifetime, *amigo*."

It was Mateo who let him know of Annie's marriage and move west. Then, as childhood friends often did over time, they fell out of touch. "What're you doing riding with Nathan Bonet?"

"I had to see for myself what kind of man *mi amigo* had become." Hank heard sadness in his friend's voice. "I know *su padre* was a mean man, but he deserved better than being stabbed in his own bed."

Mateo was right. If that was truly how his father had died, he deserved justice. But they were looking in the wrong place. "You've been lied to, old friend. There's no way my knife could have killed him when I've got it right here, strapped to my leg."

"The knife that was used to murder my brother is locked up in the sheriff's office in

Laramie," Nathan shouted. "It has your initials carved into it. We all saw it."

"Initials are easy to forge," Hank said. "If I'd wanted to kill Thomas Bonet, I'd have given him a chance to defend himself. Only a coward stabs a man while he's passed out in bed." Though nothing had been said to that effect, Hank had no doubt of it. "You take me for a coward, Mateo?"

"Not the *Enojado* I remember," he answered. "Are you saying somebody set you up?"

"Looks that way, *amigo*."

"We know what we saw," Nathan shouted, impatience growing in his voice. "You can't talk yourself out of this one, half-breed."

"Now hold on, Nathan," Hank heard Mateo say. "Maybe there's some truth to his claim. Maybe he was set up."

"Are you questioning me?" Nathan asked.

Hank's blood cooled. An instant later a gunshot reverberated off the cliff, and he knew Mateo Blake, the scrawny half-Mexican kid who had befriended him when nobody else would, had paid for his mistake.

"You other men comfortable with that?" Hank shouted harshly. "Blake was a good man."

"Just come on out of there and nothing will happen."

Hank did not recognize the voice, but he heard the unease in it. "You don't believe that any more than I do. You best get while you can. Once night falls, none of you are leaving this mountain alive."

~~~

Clouds had begun to roll in by the time Alice and Pete saddled their horses and headed out. Pete wore his woolen coat, Alice the oversized broadcloth that belonged to her pa. She had her own coat of course, one that fit better, but wearing her pa's gave her comfort. She appreciated that Pete wasn't the talkative sort, the kind that felt a need to fill the silence with the sound of his own voice. Alice preferred silence. It allowed a body to hear the call of a robin in the trees, the sough of a light breeze through the aspens at the creek's edge, the water a constant backdrop of rippling and bubbling over rocks worn smooth.

The horses grazed in small bunches, some nursing their foals. A few had already bedded down for the night.

After a time, Pete said, "I hope to have a place like this some day," as if more to himself than anybody else.
~~~

"Why didn't your pa give you the house and land when they left?"

"They needed a grubstake to get set up back east. I've got a cache I'm workin' on."

"It had to be a hard decision, staying behind," Alice said. "This girl you're sweet on, she anybody I know?"

"Her name's Margaret Kenner. She works at the restaurant."

"Is she the tall, skinny one with dark brown hair?"

Pete laughed. "That's her. She's got some filling out to do, I'll admit. But she has a way about her..."

Alice smiled at the sappy look that came over his face. "She sounds nice."

They drew up to the section of fence she and Uncle Hank had replaced. Seeing their handiwork made her worry about him all the more.

She tucked deeper into her coat. It was going to get cold tonight in the mountains. "We should head back."

Pete nodded. "It'll be dark soon."

As they turned their horses, Alice thought she heard the faint echo of a report in the distance. Her heart froze. She saw Pete look to the mountains. "You heard it too," she said.

He turned away. "A hunter, that's all."

Alice held back the sharp reply balanced on the tip of her tongue. She had made up her mind not to argue with him anymore. He was a man of his word and she would not ask him to be less. "You're probably right."

But she'd seen the worry in Pete's eyes. He didn't believe what he said any more than she did.

Alice was more certain now than ever that her uncle had taken to the hills. She only hoped he hadn't been at the receiving end of that shot.

Chapter 9

Hank added wood to the small fire. While he waited for the coffee to boil, he rolled the carved figure Pete gave him in his hand. A dog, he decided. The legs were too short for a wolf.

"What do you think?" he asked his horse. "Should I call him Lucky?"

The palomino appeared not to hear and continued eating on the handful of grain Hank had given him.

"You're right," Hank said. "It should be something more creative, like Cordelia or Penelope. I haven't decided on a name for you, either. How about Daffodil?"

The horse whickered and gave his head a shake. Hank laughed. "I agree. Daffodil is not a proper name for a fine stud such as yourself. It deserves more thought."

The fact that he was considering a name for a horse had Hank shaking his own head as well. It was the girl. Alice had him thinking on things a drifting man wouldn't have given the time of day. It was not an unpleasant feeling.

He leaned back and enjoyed an apple while the coffee pot came to a boil. His canteens were full and his saddlebags stocked with grub, thanks to Alice. He and his horse would stay warm and well fed. If it weren't for the men waiting to shoot him as soon as he poked his head out of the cave, he could have holed up a week or more with ease. He'd like that some day, to spend his time without any concerns beyond seeing to simple needs. Food and water. A good horse. A roof over his head. A soft bed and somebody who cared about him at his side.

Somebody with yellow hair and pretty green eyes.

He tossed another stick on the fire, sending a small eruption of sparks into the air, and muttered, "You're a dreamer, Henry Bonet." He had a woman who cared for him once, in Mexico, a woman with long black hair and eyes to match.

A stray bullet from a drunk took her life. Hank showed no mercy avenging her death.

Once it was over, he left Mexico, the taste of revenge raw in his mouth.

He thought he had put enough distance and years between himself and that taste. Then those men attempted to harm Alice during the race in Baker City, and his need for revenge returned. He saw now it was a taste he'd never distance, not as long as there was someone left in his life to care for.

El Enojado. The name fit.

He knew what needed doing come dark. The dice had been tossed. Two men were already dead, one of them a friend. Did Mateo have a wife and children waiting for him back in Laramie? The needless loss saddened Hank.

He tucked Lucky – for he did not have his niece's imagination to come up with a better name – into his shirt pocket, sipped his coffee, and waited.

~~~

Alice went to the root cellar and brought up the jar of dried herbs her ma used to make tea when Pa had trouble sleeping. It contained valerian and chamomile, and a couple other medicinal herbs with names she could not remember. Herbs her ma brought west with her and used sparingly. One spoonful always put Pa right to sleep, and he'd wake in the
~~~

morning feeling "fit as a fiddle," he liked to say.

If one spoonful made a man sleep through the night, would a double dose buy her a few more hours? Or would it make him sick, maybe even kill him? Alice didn't know. Ma use to warn that just because a little of something was good didn't make a lot of it better. Did that include Pa's sleeping tonic?

It smelled awful, that much Alice knew for sure. She measured a heaping spoonful into the china teapot and poured boiling water over it. Then she took the jar of crystallized honey off the shelf. The hoarded sweetener made everything taste better than it smelled.

~~~

Nightfall brought a cold, hard rain. Hank thought of the narrow path outside the cave, not much more than loose dirt and rock. A man might survive a slide from an unstable hillside, but what of his horse? He had planned to let Nathan and his men bring the fight to him, pick them off one by one. But the weather and his temperament changed that. The way he saw it, he had a better chance of getting himself and the palomino out of this in one piece if he forced their hand and didn't give them time to collect their wits.

He downed the last of the coffee in the pot,
~~~

packed his gear, and saddled the palomino, then kicked dirt over the fire, throwing the cave into darkness. Once his eyes adjusted, he drew his side arm and led his horse to the mouth of the cave. Rain spat off the rocks and rushed through the trees. Nothing else stirred. Hank holstered his gun and mounted up. He'd come at them quiet.

The palomino chose its steps with care, hugging the side of the hill so close Hank's knee dug a groove in the muddy bank, soaking the leg of his pants. A steady, cold stream of rainwater ran from the brim of his hat and cut his ability to see much beyond the nose of his horse. The trail looked longer in the dark. Or maybe his impatience made it seem that way.

They rounded a natural curve in the hillside, and the glow of a campfire broke the darkness. Two men sat around it. One may have been Nathan, but Hank could not be certain. The shadow of a man, no doubt sent to guard the trail, stood up, blocking the way. The palomino reared its head and stopped. Hank drew the rifle to his shoulder and pulled the trigger. His horse flicked its ears, but held its ground.

The shadow answered with a burst of pistol flame. The bullet cut the hillside at

Hank's shoulder. Hank fired again. The shadow grunted and fell out of sight. Hank had no way of telling who it was. He hoped it had not been Nathan, for they had unfinished business.

The campfire, now abandoned, came back into view. Hank kicked the palomino into action, knowing a man riding a white horse against a dark hillside made an easy target.

The remaining two men were apparently night blind, having been caught staring at the fire, for their first shots missed, sending dirt and rock in Hank's face. Hank rode half-blind himself, trusting the palomino to get them to solid ground in one piece. He fired at the gun bursts, but from a moving horse, he had no delusions of hitting anything.

They reached the trailhead and a bullet whipped by his cheek.

"I want him alive!" Nathan shouted.

Good, Hank thought, then the palomino danced sideways of a sudden, catching him off guard and throwing him from the saddle. He lost his rifle, scrambled to get free of the horse's hooves and to get his feet under him. He feared his horse had been shot, but the palomino regained its legs and ran into the trees.

From a crouch, Hank drew his pistol and

fired without a clear target. An answering bullet fractured the rock near his hand, embedding a shard in the meat of his thumb. He lost his grip on the pistol. The heel of his boot kicked out from under him, sending him belly first in the mud. Again he tried to stand, but the ground shifted beneath him. He scrabbled for a handhold. The embankment gave way and he rode the landslide over the edge.

~~~

Pete's loud, steady snoring competed with the rain hammering the barn's tin roof. Relieved she had not killed him by insisting he drink a second cup of tea, Alice clutched her small canvas tote of supplies under her slicker and made her way to the stalls, her only light the fractured glow from the potbelly stove. She took care to move quietly as she saddled Penny.

She packed light, intending to travel fast: tinder box, biscuit and bacon sandwiches, water, rope, the beaded leather medicine bag that had belonged to Grandma Ela. Uncle Hank had more than enough supplies for the two of them if she found him. And if she didn't, she'd come back and put together a search party. She could not sleep, could not go on about her life, without knowing he was all
~~~

right. She'd stood by helpless to do anything when little Joey and Ma and then Pa died. She refused to stand by helpless this time.

Alice hoped Nan did not worry over-much about her. And she hoped Pete did not think bad of her for leaving him to shoulder the responsibilities of the ranch on his own. Though she didn't know him well, she had no doubt he'd keep his end of their agreement. She prayed the Great Spirit was on her side, that he would guide her, but she was going to find her uncle, with or without the Great Spirit's help.

~~~

Hank's foot caught on a branch protruding from the hillside, arresting his descent. Before he could draw a breath, the branch snapped and he was sliding again. He made a grab for the branch stub as it ripped through the front of his coat. His fingers slipped on thick mud and he continued to drop into the darkness. In an effort to slow his fall, he yanked out handfuls of vines, clawed at clumps of brush that slapped his face and knocked his hat off.

His knee smashed into an outcropping of loose rock that crumbled under the impact and sent him flying backwards. He flailed, legs and arms grabbing and kicking at a black void,
~~~

then rocks and mud, then emptiness again. Falling debris clogged his mouth and throat as he bounced and tumbled down the hill like a sack of potatoes.

He struck a boulder broadside and jolted to a halt, dazed, unable to draw a breath. Rocks pelted his back and bare head. He attempted to stand, to get clear of the falling debris. The ground shifted beneath his feet and he lost his balance, fell again, striking his shoulder on the same unforgiving boulder. He scrambled on all fours, sharp rocks and branches tearing at his hands and knees. His bruised ribcage and shoulder screamed at him to stop, but he'd be buried alive if he didn't keep going.

A pair of legs appeared in front of him, and a hand grabbed the back of his coat. "You're not getting away from me that easy," Nathan Bonet said.

~~~

Alice headed for the one place she knew to be a good hideout and shelter – a cave far back and high in the timber. With luck, Uncle Hank had found it and was holed up there. She could not make out the trail in the dark, but it didn't matter. She had ridden it many times and remembered the way by heart. The relentless rain made for slow, slippery going. She resisted
~~~

the urge to risk her horse coming up lame by becoming impatient and carelessness.

Emerging from a grove of aspen, she and Penny crossed the meadow where Alice and her ma use to pick yarrow for healing tinctures and wildflowers for the table. Ma always chose the bluebells when they were in bloom. Later Pa would come in for supper, snatch the jar of flowers up and present them to Ma like he was courting her. Laughing, she'd set the jar back on the table and tell him to go pick his own flowers. He always replied with a loud kiss that made Alice blush and little Joey giggle.

Cold aloneness seeped into Alice's bones. Her uncle's words came back to her. *Go on best you can. Make a good life for yourself.*

She hardened her face against crying and rode on.

~~~

Nathan dragged Hank clear of the slide. "I'm taking you back to Wyoming to hang for the murder of my brother."

Hank labored to breathe. Every battered inch of his body ached as though he'd been worked over by a prize fighter and lost. His hands were raw and swollen; the gash in his right palm bled mud stained red. He attempted to get his feet under him, but could not make
~~~

his weak legs support his weight. Nathan yanked him upright; Hank went for the Bowie strapped at his leg, but his swollen fingers were unable to grip the handle.

"I'll take that," Nathan said, slapping Hank's hand away. He drew the knife from its sheathe and tucked it under his belt.

"What will you do if I'm found innocent?"

Nathan grunted. "Not much chance of that."

Hank knew he spoke the truth. Without his Bowie as proof, it would be his word against the word of a white man. And that white man possessed his only evidence.

Nathan hauled him over to a dun, lashed his hands together with a length of rope, and said, "Keep up or be dragged."

"Will watching me hang clear your guilty conscience?"

"I have no conscience."

He tied the other end of the rope to his saddle horn and mounted. The dun began walking. Hank staggered a few paces before falling to his knees. He rolled onto his back, held his head up out of the mud as best he could, while stones and roots tore at his coat, bruised his shoulders and gouged his back. Before long, the last of his strength played out, and he faded into a black, pain-filled world.

~~~

When Hank came to, he found himself back at the grassy clearing, sitting propped against a tree. His bound hands were tied to the tree's trunk by a short length of rope. His hair hung in his face and mud covered him from head to boots. His cut palm bled through a makeshift neckerchief binding. Little remained of his shredded coat, and he shivered against the persistent, cold rain.

By the light of the fire, he saw Nathan pulling up camp, as though preparing to leave and take the dead men's horses and gear with him. The body sprawled a yard from the fire looked to be Mateo Blake. The body of the man Hank shot at the trailhead lay where he fell.

"You got Pierce there in the neck as you went over the bank," Nathan said, nodding toward a third body a few feet away. "Lucky shot."

Hank saw nothing lucky about it. Four men were dead because of Nathan Bonet. "You knew they'd learn the truth once you caught up with me. You never intended for any of them to make it back alive, did you."

"Nobody in Laramie liked my brother," Nathan answered with cold matter-of-factness.
~~~

"I couldn't risk a sympathetic judge letting you off because you'd done the community a favor. Those other men though, they had families. They won't take kindly to hearing their men are dead."

Troubled by the senseless grief Nathan's actions stood to bring to innocent wives and children, Hank asked, "Why is it so important to you that I hang?"

"I have my reasons," was all the answer he got.

"Blake deserves a proper burial. If we stay here until morning, I'll see to it, along with those others."

Nathan grunted. "You're in no shape to be digging holes." He continued gathering gear. "That horse of yours is probably halfway back to the Calder ranch by now. If we stay 'til morning, this place'll be overrun with folks looking for you. Maybe even that niece of ours. Alice."

At the mention of Alice's name, bile rose in Hank's throat. "Stay away from her."

"As long as she keeps her distance, I've no quarrel with the girl." Nathan led a charcoal gelding over. "Since you and Blake were such good buddies, you can have his horse." He hauled Hank to his feet and muscled him into the saddle.

Sharp pain stabbed through Hank's bruised middle. He took shallow breaths to keep from blacking out. It didn't feel as though any ribs were broken, but close to it.

Well before daybreak, they left camp. Nathan rode ahead, leading the gelding. Hank's hands were lashed to the horn of Blake's worn-out saddle, his feet bound by a short rope under the gelding's belly. The remaining three horses followed in a string behind.

Hank thought he saw the palomino watching like a ghost through the trees, but could not be certain. The stallion would eventually make its way back to the ranch, as Nathan said. Alice would think him hurt or dead and come looking for him, but there was nothing he could do about it now. For the moment, his fate was in another man's hands.

Chapter 10

A weak gray dawn had begun to stain the sky when Alice came upon a slide of mud and rock blocking her trail. The rain had stopped, but fat, soaking drops continued to fall from the tree limbs. She looked up, the wide brim of her hat shielding her eyes. The slide started near where she guessed the cave's trailhead to be. Despair came over her. If her uncle had taken shelter there, his only way out now may be straight down.

She scanned the hillside just beyond the slide and spotted something large lodged in the branches of a tree. Moving closer, she realized it was a man's body. He wore dark trousers and a broadcloth coat. Fear closed Alice's throat. Heart thudding in her ears, she nudged Penny to the opposite side of the tree for a better look.

The man had light-colored hair.

Not Uncle Hank.

Alice sucked in a relieved breath. She forced herself to look closer at the man's face, his mouth frozen in a grimace, his eyes open and glazed over, impervious to the cold and wet. Stubble covered his cheeks, but she saw no scar.

Not Nathan Bonet, either.

Who was he then? How'd he get there?

His hanging in the tree set Alice's nerves dancing. Her gaze swung back to the pile of mud and rock blocking the trail. She didn't think it likely the slide had thrown the man such a distance. Had anyone been on the bank when it gave way? What if there was another body, one buried under the debris, maybe still alive?

Uncle Hank, where are you?

Alice pulled her rifle free and dismounted. She didn't know if the dead man had been alone, didn't know who else may be nearby, willed herself to stand her ground and slowly survey her surroundings.

Movement in the trees brought the rifle to her shoulder, looking for a target.

Uncle Hank's palomino stepped out, reins

trailing. He tossed his head and snorted. Penny whickered in answer. Alice took slow, deep breaths to quiet her pulse, and slid the rifle back into its boot.

The palomino moved closer. Alice pulled off a glove and extended her hand, palm up. "It's all right," she said softly. "You know me."

He flicked his ears and came to her, planted his soft muzzle in her palm.

"Good boy."

Alice caressed his neck with her free hand and continued to murmur gently, let him nuzzle her palm until she felt certain he would allow her to examine him. Pulling off her other glove, she checked his legs for cuts or swelling, ran her hands over his shoulders, sides, rump, then under the saddle blanket. He appeared unharmed. The rifle boot was empty but the saddlebags full, bedroll tied in place. Her uncle had been on the move before something happened to leave his horse without its rider.

Alice looked to the landslide again. Maybe the two things – the landslide and her uncle missing – had nothing to do with each other, but she didn't think that the case.

And what about the dead man in the tree?

The palomino nudged her shoulder. Alice looked him in the eye. "Do you know where he is?"

The horse tossed its head – away from the debris, thankfully – toward the trail to the cave.

Alice looped his reins around the saddle horn so he wouldn't stumble on them. "Show me."

The palomino started up the trail. Alice gathered Penny's reins, climbed into the saddle, and followed. She knew she should go back to the ranch for help. The farther she rode in the opposite direction, the more her conscience nagged her like Mrs. Henderson at the mercantile.

But another feeling nagged at her worse, the feeling that Uncle Hank was in danger, possibly hurt. Returning to the ranch meant losing a day or more, time he may not have.

And there was the palomino. If she went back, she'd have to take him with her, and he'd lose the scent. Horses didn't track the way a dog did. Her ma taught her that. She said *Hinono'eino*, "our people," had used horses to find buffalo herds. A horse smelled the air, could follow a scent with two feet of snow on the ground. But their range was limited.

As long as the palomino detected a scent, Alice would follow and hope he led her to her uncle.

They climbed the trail through the dripping trees until they'd reached the edge of the grassy flat to the cave. The palomino shied, refused to move any closer. Penny's skin quivered and she stopped beside him. Alice's breath caught at the sight of three more men, all lying dead: one sprawled next to a cold fire, another on his back a short distance away, the third at what remained of the trailhead.

She dismounted, pulled the Winchester from its boot, and went to the man by the fire. Swallowing against the urge to throw up, she grabbed a handful of thick black hair and lifted his head. No scar. The other two men didn't have a scar on their faces either. Four dead men altogether, their gear and horses gone. Nathan Bonet must still be alive. How did her uncle fit in all this? Where was he?

She stepped as close as she dared to the unstable trailhead and shouted in the direction of the cave, "Uncle Hank, are you here?"

Silence.

She tried once more, louder. "Uncle Hank?"

There came no reply. Alice turned away and saw a pistol lying near the edge of the slide. She picked it up and recognized her uncle's Colt revolver. A cold chill coursed through her. Four men dead and Uncle Hank missing. Did the man with the scarred face have him? And if so, why?

Alice looked at the death around her. What kind of man leaves his partners to rot? Uncle Hank told her to shoot Nathan Bonet on sight. Until she made sense of it all, she'd do best to watch her back.

~~~

They rode the high, rocky ridge of a canyon cut by a white-capped river, its water churned brown from erosion. A slanting, cold rain drove through Hank's ripped coat, ached through his bruised chest, numbed his hands and legs. Mud washed from his hair and into his eyes. He missed his hat. Blake's slicker, tied to the bedroll behind him and out of reach of his bound hands, served only as an irritant. Blinking through the mud, he stared at Nathan's straight back, the water rolling off his fur sombrero and black mackintosh. If the man felt any discomfort, he did not show it.

Hank harbored little doubt that Nathan killed Thomas Bonet. Nathan laying hands on Thomas's wife had been but one of many times Hank saw the brothers fight. It was no stretch to imagine either of them crossing a line that could not be uncrossed. That Nathan went to the trouble of framing Hank meant a fair
~~~

amount of planning had gone into the killing. Hank wondered if he'd merely been an easy scapegoat – the murdered man's estranged son returning to settle a score – or if there was more to it.

It was a long ride to Laramie. Hank planned to have some answers before getting that far.

After a time the rain quit. They descended into the sage-covered canyon and stopped among a cluster of stunted spruce at the bank of the river. Nathan untied Hank's ankles, loosened the rope binding his hands to the saddle horn, and pulled him to the ground.

Hank collapsed, his numb legs unable to support him. Pain shot through his chest and robbed his breath. Nathan hauled him to a tree, where he was once again tied by a short lead and his feet re-bound.

Nathan threw Blake's slicker across his shoulders almost as an afterthought. "Can't have you dying of a chill before we get there," he remarked.

"You want to keep me alive, let me change into something dry."

"Haven't got time," Nathan said. "Soon as we've eaten, we move on, put as much distance as possible between us and whoever might be following before nightfall." He set the horses on a long lead to graze and drink, then began gathering firewood.

Hank took stock of his condition. His bruised ribs were tolerable if he drew shallow breaths. Being hauled from his horse had not helped matters. The neckerchief wrapped around the wound to his hand was soaked. He couldn't be certain how much of it was from the rain and how much was blood. His frozen fingers ached; he stuck them between his thighs for warmth. His wounds would heal, if the cold and wet didn't do him in first.

When Nathan had a small fire kindled, Hank asked, "Was he drunk when you killed him?"

Nathan smirked. "You're pretty sure I did it."

"I am. What I don't know is why."

"Does it matter?"

"If I'm to hang for it, it does."

"All right then." Nathan put the coffee pot on to boil and rocked back on his heels. "That piece of land Tom owns...*owned*," he corrected, "is in the middle of cattle country. The surrounding ranchers offered enough money to set both of us up for life, but my lazy drunk of a brother refused to sell. It made a lot of cattlemen angry." He spat. "If I hadn't killed him, one of them would have."

Hank had heard of it happening to other landowners, their families threatened or murdered over grazing rights. Little Medicine Bow River flowed through the western edge of his father's property, a prime water source any cattleman would covet. "So you hurried things along and framed me for his murder. With me out of the way, the land becomes yours."

Nathan gave a smile that did not suit the look in his eyes. "There is Alice to consider. She may take a notion her granddaddy's land belongs to her."

Hank's stomach tightened. "Touch her and I'll – "

Nathan laughed. "You'll what? You can barely sit a horse." He went back to preparing grub. "Like I said before, as long as she stays clear of Wyoming Territory, I have no quarrel with her. If she doesn't," he paused as though thinking it over, then shrugged and said, "so be it."

He had killed his own brother; a half-breed girl was nothing to him. He said it himself, he has no conscience. Alice would never be safe as long as Nathan Bonet lived. Sickened by the thought, desperate to prevent harm coming to his niece, Hank said, "I want nothing to do with that land. Give me a piece of paper to sign and it's yours."

Nathan set the fry pan down and brought his face close. "It's not that simple." Hank saw the hardness in his eyes, smelled the bitterness in him. "It's not nearly that simple."

~~~

Alice crested the ridge of Burnt River canyon. She'd never been this far east before but had heard stories of how difficult the canyon was for wagons to navigate. The river and its tributaries were said to be rich with gold.

She'd made the decision to find her uncle. His saddlebags held everything she needed for a long ride: food, a small cook pot, fry skillet and coffee pot, matches wrapped in oilcloth, two fifty-round boxes of .44-40s, same as her Winchester took. Uncle Hank's blankets and clothes were rolled in a tarpaulin and tied behind his saddle. Two canteens of water hung from the saddle horn.

The palomino followed the trail of at least five horses. Judging by the depth of the tracks, two of the horses carried men. Those men had to be Uncle Hank and Nathan Bonet. Alice didn't believe her uncle would leave his gun
~~~

and horse behind by choice, which meant Nathan Bonet must be holding him against his will. She had no way of knowing why or what his intentions were. Pete mentioned family business. Were they headed to Laramie?

Wyoming Territory. To reach it, she'd have to cross Idaho Territory. If she didn't catch up with the riders soon, the palomino would lose her uncle's scent, leaving it up to her to find the trail. Ma and Pa taught her the ways of tracking, not just how to identify different prints and scat – rabbit, deer, bear – but of other signs to look for as well. Two men and five horses needed to stop for food and rest, leaving behind campfire ashes, horse droppings, human droppings, broken branches. It was likely they didn't know they were being followed and would make no effort to hide their tracks.

Yet doubt tugged at Alice. If she stuck close to the route her folks had traveled to reach Oregon, she'd have to cross the Snake River. French-Canadian trappers called its wild rapids, falls, and cascades *accursed*. A ferry had taken Ma and Pa's wagon and horses safely across the Snake at the border into Oregon. But there'd been another crossing farther into Idaho, where three islands broke the river into narrow channels, the crossing where her Grandma Ela had drowned.

Ma and Pa's wagon was halfway across the second channel when a bucket broke loose. Grandma Ela reached for it, lost her balance and went over the side. The swift river sucked her under the wagon.

"Joseph jumped in to rescue her," Ma said, "but he couldn't find her. He was a strong swimmer, but the current was too swift even for him. If it not for the wagon master's quick thinking and practiced hand with a lasso, Joseph would have drowned too." Ma always cried when she got to that part of the story. "I lost my mother and nearly became a widow that day."

The memory ached through Alice's heart. "Great Spirit, if you're riding with me, let me find Uncle Hank before we get to that crossing."

~~~

Sometime later, Alice jerked awake, gripped the saddle horn and tightened her knees into Penny's sides to keep from falling. She looked around at the rocky hillside, disoriented. The cold rain had stopped, and the horses had made their way into Burnt River canyon. The palomino grazed at the bank of
~~~

the river, next to the remains of a campfire. Alice couldn't be certain how old it was, what with the recent rain, but the fact that the palomino had been the one to find it gave her hope that her uncle had come through here.

Might be the scent of someone else, but she chose not to believe so.

Sleep pulled at Alice's eyelids. "I need coffee." She dismounted, tethered the horses, and took her uncle's hatchet to get firewood.

A dead tree lie a short distance away. She chopped a thick branch off and held the cut end to her cheek. The center was dry. She gathered an armload of smaller limbs and built a base with them, split and crossed over one another. Taking her pa's folding knife, she skived the bark and wet wood from the larger branch until she reached the dry center, then made fine shavings for tinder.

As she worked, she heard her ma's gentle voice guide her patiently through each step. When the char cloth ignited and flames took hold of the shavings, Alice added more tinder, then kindling, until she had a bright flame substantial enough to warm her hands and heat a pot of coffee. While she waited for the water to boil, she ate one of the bacon sandwiches she'd made for her uncle and stared into the flames licking at the wood.

When she jerked awake the next time, night had fallen. The uneaten remains of her sandwich lay in her lap, and the fire had dwindled to a small pile of embers. The palomino slept standing nearby, eyes closed, lower lip hanging loose. On the other side of him, Penny did the same.

~~~

Nathan pushed hard after their midday break, pausing only briefly to spell the horses. Hank judged they'd covered another twelve miles by the time they stopped for the night and Nathan set up camp.

"You look to be about Pierce's size," he said, went to a long-legged black gelding and took down the bedroll. Inside was a blue flannel shirt, a pair of denim pants, socks and long underwear. He released Hank's bindings and stepped back, resting his hand on the butt of the pistol at his hip. "Make it quick."

Hank's cold fingers fumbled with the buttons of his ripped shirt. As he pulled it off, he was surprised to find Pete's carved dog – *Lucky* – lodged in the pocket. He palmed the figure, masked transferring it to the dry shirt's pocket behind a stab of pain; his bruised ribcage protested as he worked his arms into
~~~

the blue flannel. The shirt smelled of sweat and horse but fit well enough.

He released the straps of his empty knife sheath to remove his wet trousers. Nathan grabbed it up. "You'll get this back when we ride into Laramie."

Hank couldn't see that it made much difference, as long as the knife it belonged to remained in Nathan's possession. But he said nothing.

Pierce's underwear was stained with piss but dry. Hank put them on. The legs of the denim pants stopped short of Hank's ankles; long socks filled the gap. He managed to shove his feet into his damp boots, but the effort broke open the wound to his hand. "I need a clean neckerchief," he said.

Nathan tossed him one of his own. Once Hank wrapped his wound, he had no choice but to put his tattered coat back on. Nor was there a spare hat to be had. At least he had Blake's slicker to cut the wind and rain. When he was finished, Nathan re-bound his hands and feet.

Little was said between them over a meal of hardtack and rice with salt pork. Hank's battered body throbbed, deep, and he resigned himself to never being warm again, in spite of the dry clothing. Later, as he lay beneath the covers and stared up at the tarpaulin shelter, he ached for the relief of unconsciousness. But his mind would not rest while his father's murderer slept nearby.

Nathan killed his brother out of anger and jealousy, much as Cain had killed Abel in the Holy Bible. Hank didn't put much stock in the teachings of a Christian god, but he knew the stories. Oftentimes a worn bible had been the only book around to read on a cold night. Cain showed no remorse for what he'd done, nor did Nathan Bonet. Hank doubted the man knew the meaning of the word. God had banished Cain to a life as a restless wanderer, unable to produce crops from the soil he had desecrated with Abel's blood. Hank did not know Nathan's future, but he knew the man would never shed the stain of his brother's blood on his hands, regardless of what a court decided.

Hank tested the rope binding his wrists. The fibers bit into his flesh, held tight. The tether was just long enough to allow him to roll over, but fell far short of reaching the man sleeping scant feet away. Nathan Bonet knew to take no chances.

And with good reason, Hank thought. He

would be patient, give his body time to heal. Wait for Nathan to make a mistake. Men driven by jealousy always did.

Chapter 11

Alice had no choice but to string up a makeshift cover and bed down until daybreak. She struck camp at first light and let the palomino have his head, but he was more interested in grazing than tracking, and Alice knew he'd lost her uncle's scent.

"Weren't your fault," she told the horse. "If I hadn't fallen asleep..." But she knew she was being unfair to herself. The horses had needed the rest as much as she had. She clipped a lead to the palomino's halter and mounted up. Tracking was on her now.

She followed the river eastward and found where several hooves had churned the mud at the bank. The weather held, and at midday they came upon the remains of another camp: a cold fire doused by coffee grounds, a charred food tin, flattened grass and twigs between two trees where the men had no doubt slept under a shelter, and the droppings of several horses near the water's edge.

Alice stayed long enough to work her way through a strip of beef jerky and let her horses graze and drink, then pressed on.

Two days later, they left the canyon and crossed a sage-covered valley to the Snake River, the border between Oregon and Idaho Territory. The sun broke through the clouds and glistened off its surface; thick cables spanned the river's breadth. The ferry was a fenced-in wooden platform with a loading ramp, a smaller platform and pulley wheel off to one side.

A big man stuffed into a bearskin coat squinted at her as though his eyesight was failing, his leathery face hidden behind a mass of white beard stained brown. "Afternoon," he called. "You lookin' to cross?"

"That depends," Alice replied. "Did a couple men with a string of horses come through here?"

"Early this morning. You know 'em?"

"One's my uncle."

"Would he be the half-breed or the disagreeable hombre with a scar on his face?"

"My uncle is half Arapaho."

The ferryman shook his head, spat a stream of tobacco juice over the railing. "He didn't look too well off, like he'd been worked over before the other fella tied him to his horse."

Her fears confirmed, Alice asked, "Did this other fellow say where they were headed?"

"He wasn't the talkative sort, 'cept for cussin' about the crossing fee. Fifty cents for a rider and horse," he told her. "Plus two bits for the packhorse."

If the palomino stallion objected to be called a packhorse, he didn't let on. Alice dug the coins from her pocket and led him and Penny aboard.

"Mighty disagreeable, that hombre," the big man grumbled, as he closed the gate across the end of the ferry.

Alice did her best to ignore the misgivings his words stirred. She'd come too far to change her mind now. She secured the horses to the railing as the ferryman stepped out onto the small platform and set the pulley wheel in motion.

The ferry glided into the current, and the lines holding it to the cables stretched taut. A chill wind tugged at Alice's hat brim. The motion of the platform beneath her feet was a new experience and took some adjusting to, the water high and swift. She braced herself as it slapped the bottom of the ferry.

Penny shied at the unfamiliar sound. "Easy, girl," Alice said, and put a reassuring hand on the horse's neck. The palomino stood calm, as though this wasn't a new experience for him.

They neared the middle of the river, and it occurred to Alice that she was seeing the same things her ma and pa would have seen when they traveled west, only in reverse. The bank ahead, butted against a basalt cliff, was where they'd have driven their wagon to wait for the ferry – if not this one, one just like it. She turned and looked at the opposite bank. Where she had loaded, they would have disembarked, entered Oregon for the first time, and continued to Baker City.

The river looked even bigger from the middle, something to be respected. She tried to imagine what it must have felt like to make the crossing in a covered wagon heavy with everything you owned. To suffer losses and find the strength to continue. Some distance upriver was where her grandma had drowned.

For the first time, the enormity of what folks moving west endured – not just her ma and pa, but everyone who settled in Baker City and places beyond, like Portland – became more than stories told around the table. Their courage and determination humbled Alice.

Too soon, the ferry bumped against the opposite shore and its operator secured the pulley wheel. "Glenn's Ferry is about a four-day ride from here," he said and opened the ramp gates. "Unless the fellas you're tracking have business in Boise, be my guess that's where they're headed."

"Appreciate it," Alice said.

"Watch your back," he offered as she unloaded the horses.

"I intend to."

~~~

The Snake River carved a wide, bow-shaped depression through the basalt plains of southwestern Idaho Territory. With every mile they put behind them, Hank felt the sickness grow in his lungs. His chest pain worsened, and he fought against coughing. When he could no longer avoid it, he doubled over and expelled rust-colored sputum. By the time they reached Glenn's Ferry, he burned with fever.

"Tom told me about your mother drowning somewhere around here," Nathan said as they crossed to the southern bank of the river.
~~~

"Funny," he gave a mirthless laugh, "I thought all you injuns could swim."

Hank said nothing in response, for the comment deserved none. When Annie's letter found him thirteen years ago, giving him the news of their mother's death, a month had already transpired. He had railed at the injustice of it, her finally being free of Thomas Bonet and not surviving long enough to enjoy it. Years of regret piled on him for not making an effort to see her before she was gone.

Just as he'd done with Annie.

His sister's letter said Joe planted a marker some distance from the bank, even though they never found her body, but Hank saw no evidence of one. Weather and time had most likely returned it to the soil from which it came.

Now a ferry, large enough to take two wagons and teams of oxen at a time, safely crossed the wide expanse. Hank's bitterness deepened, along with the sickness in his lungs.

~~~

The weather remained dry, though gray and cold. Alice gaped at smooth boulders the size of barns strewn across the river's canyon, as though they'd been rolled there from some distant place; the *kee-kee-kee-kee* of a prairie
~~~

falcon echoed off the canyon walls. Where the land flattened, enormous shallow basins so symmetrical they looked manmade ringed miles of sagebrush.

The trail she followed gave wide berth to the rare settlement or homestead, skirted south of Boise just as the ferryman predicted. What was Nathan Bonet hiding, that he'd go out of his way to avoid people? Alice wondered. What were his intentions? The big man in the bearskin coat told her Uncle Hank had looked worked over. How hurt was he?

The only way to find out was to catch up with her uncle and the man holding him against his will. Urgency gnawed at her, but she resisted pushing the horses any harder; she needed them more than they needed her.

Shortly before reaching Glenn's Ferry, she stopped to relieve herself, and came upon a wooden marker, grayed by weather, partially hidden in a clump of sagebrush. She pushed the brush aside and read the roughly carved words, put there by her pa with the pocket knife she now carried. *Beloved mother, Ela "Earth Follower" Bonet, DOB unknown, drowned August 14, 1867.*

An unexpected wave of loss cascaded through Alice, drove her to her knees. She cried for the grandmother she never had the chance to meet; she cried for her ma and pa and little Joey, cold in their graves, for Uncle Hank, held captive, injured.

And she cried for herself. What made her think she could find her uncle in all this vastness? What did she think she was going to do if she came face to face with Nathan Bonet? Did she have the courage to shoot him, if called for?

More questions. All she had was a bunch of questions with no answers. While she chased after uncertainty, the ranch needed her. The ranch was all she had, the one solid thing she could be sure of in her life.

The thought did nothing to ease her grief; the ranch was but four empty walls without her family.

Penny stepped close, nudged Alice's shoulder. Alice gripped the leather harness and let the horse help her to her feet. She hugged Penny's neck, drew comfort from her friend's reassuring warmth – *solid* – then climbed into the saddle and took up the palomino's lead. "Let's go find Uncle Hank."

A short while later, they reached Glenn's Ferry, much larger than the first one they'd ridden, the Snake River wider here, angrier.

Again Alice asked the operator about two men and a string of horses. Again she was told she'd missed them by half a day. She hadn't gained on them, but she hadn't fallen back, either.

"The one you say is your uncle was bad off," the ferryman told her, "sickly. I offered there's a doc not far from here, but the one with the scar told me to mind my own business."

Alice thanked the man, set her jaw, and headed the horses east.

~~~

Hank lost track of the number of times he'd been pulled from the saddle, one day blurring into the next. They traveled the rims of black lava canyons south of the Snake River, the way strewn with boulders and knotted sage, passed the upper and lower Salmon Falls, violent plummets in the rain-swollen river. At some point they left the river and dropped into grasslands.

By their second or third day in the grasslands, the rains began, grew steadily heavier. Driving and relentless. Hank shivered uncontrollably, each breath a great effort. His head sat heavy on his shoulders, and pain between his eyes made it difficult to focus. Little held him in the saddle but the rope
~~~

binding his hands to the horn.

Nathan rode ahead with his shoulders hunched around his ears. He steered them toward the shelter of the lodgepole pines at the grasslands' edge. A short while later, they came to an overhang of rock and tree roots that formed a shallow cave deep enough to accommodate two men and their gear. Nathan cursed the rain and dismounted. "We'll camp here until it lets up."

Again Hank was pulled out of the saddle. A wave of nausea swept through him, and a deep, painful cough doubled him over. Nathan hauled him into the cave. An exposed tree root made a natural, stout ring, which he used to secure Hank's wrists to with a short length of rope.

"You're wasting your time," Hank said, forcing the words from his course throat.

"Sick or not, I know better than to trust you." Nathan spread a tarpaulin and made up a bed. "Get yourself warm," he ordered, then set about building a fire.

Hank ached with a cold the blankets could not ease. Bone-deep shaking brought on more coughing, thick and harsh. He was weak as a newborn pup and it scared him. He watched the flames of Nathan's miserable fire take hold and knew in his gut he wasn't going to make it to Wyoming alive.

~~~

By day Alice tracked, by night she read from Wordsworth, hoping to find comfort in the poetry her uncle enjoyed. But the memory of his smile as he read about daffodils "tossing their heads in sprightly dance" only deepened the emptiness in her heart. She cried until she was cried out, and by morning she continued tracking. She saw where the men and horses left the river and headed southeast, into grasslands, found the remains of more small fires, patches of cropped grass where the horses had grazed, hoof impressions in the soft earth.

Then the rains came. Great driving sheets that filled the low spots, washed tracks away. The temperature dropped, along with visibility. By late afternoon, Alice realized she had lost the trail. She stopped the horses, gazed around at the broad grasslands, the emptiness of it all. Everything dripped cold and wet.

She could continue toward the line of trees to the east. Was that where the men had gone? Common sense told her yes, but doubt held her back. If the men had headed north or south, even just a little in either direction, she might
~~~

not pick up their trail again. She knew how easy it was to get turned around once in the trees.

"It's foolishness to keep on when I don't know where we are," she told the horses.

If they turned back now, they could retrace their steps, follow the landmarks, find their way home. Alice was certain of it.

She was also certain she'd never see her uncle again. He had promised to return if he was able, but what if he was hurt so bad he couldn't? She may never know, if she turned back now. Even if he was dead, she'd like to see his body, take him to rest beside his sister.

"Great Spirit, tell me what to do."

A wind came up, drove the rain sideways into Alice's ear and yanked at her hat.

"Is this your way of helping?" she shouted at the sky.

The wind gusted again. The horses hung their heads in discomfort, began moving away, toward the tree line. Alice relented, following their lead. They would shelter under cover of the branches until the rain let up, then decide what to do.

Once among the trees, Alice began looking for a place to hunker down. Of a sudden, the horses lifted their noses to the air almost in unison.

Then Alice smelled it too. The smoke of a campfire.

Chapter 12

Alice dismounted and tethered the horses. There was grass to be had and they set to it, not inclined to make any noise. It would be dark soon. If the men she'd been following were responsible for the smell of burning firewood, it was unlikely they'd break camp this late in the day. She drew the Winchester from its boot, looped a canteen around her shoulder, and filled her pockets with hardtack and ammunition, prepared to take as much time as needed to scout the layout. Almost as an afterthought, she took up her ma's medicine bag.

It struck Alice then that, except for these two horses, nobody knew where she was. Uncle Hank didn't know she was following him, had ordered her not to. Nan and the boys, and Pete, they most likely guessed by now she had lit out to find her uncle, but the only way they'd know which direction she took was if Uncle Hank talked it over with them behind her back. Pete maybe. But Alice didn't think her uncle would put their new ranch hand in danger that way. Nor did she believe she was being followed. She'd kept an eye on her back trail.

If something were to happen to her, who was to know?

~~~

The smell of frying bacon aroused Hank to consciousness and stirred an urge to vomit. He made to swallow and his dry throat clicked, his tongue pasted to the roof of his mouth.

Water. I need water.

No one heard.

Pain beat against his skull like a carpenter's hammer. He opened his eyes, but it took some time for his thoughts to fall in line and piece together where he was. A fire crackled nearby, its light dancing off the packed soil and tree roots overhead. A rope tied to one of the roots bound his hands. Several blankets lay atop him. He wore a dead man's clothes soaked in his own sweat. A pocket of pitch popped in the fire and he turned his head toward the sound.
~~~

It was near dark and Nathan squatted next to the flames, tending a pan of bacon, a pot of coffee setting on a flat stone at fire's edge. He glanced at Hank, poured a cup and brought it over.

Hank tried to raise up but was too weak. Nathan propped his head and held the cup to his lips. Hank took a sip. The hot liquid loosened his tongue from the roof of his mouth and soothed his parched throat. He went for another sip and choked, began coughing. Hot coffee sloshed over Nathan's hand.

"God damn it!" Nathan stood and tossed the rest of the cup's contents aside.

Hank curled into the cough until it subsided. He didn't know which hurt worse – his bruised ribs, his lungs, or his head.

"Don't you die on me," Nathan said. "I mean to see you hang."

"Why?" Hank rasped. He knew Nathan never had any use for him, but to frame him for murder? There had to be more to it than inheriting Thomas Bonet's land. He needed to know the reason before his time came.

"I'll tell you why." Nathan leaned in close and dragged a finger down the scar on his face. "You, a half-breed brat, turned my brother against me."

Hank stared at him. "You brought that on yourself when you struck Mother."

Nathan straightened and spat. "She was a squaw who thought too high of herself. I put her in her place. And for that, I've carried the mark of my brother's disrespect like a brand."

The mark of Cain – though Nathan's mark had not been given as a sign of protection, and Thomas Bonet had not been God. "You killed him to get even."

"Don't get me wrong, that land will set me up nice, and I mean to have it. But, yes, I've waited a long time to see you pay for my disfigurement, you and Tom both."

Hank finally had the truth of it. He was destined to hang over something that happened twenty years ago. He considered informing Nathan that revenge wouldn't bring him the satisfaction he sought, but it would fall on deaf ears. Decades of bitterness had consumed any trace of humanity the man may have once possessed.

"Then get it over with," Hank said, pushing the words out. He wasn't going to make it anyhow. Better a quick end.

"Oh no." Nathan gave a vengeful smile. "I want witnesses. I want the high-minded people of Laramie to see which one of us deserves their contempt."

~~~

Alice sat on her haunches behind a sizable pine tree, just beyond the light of the fire and downwind of the horses, the Winchester across her thighs. She wasn't close enough to be seen or smelled, but with the wind being in her favor, she heard every word that passed between her uncle and the man who had him tied up like a dog.

Nathan Bonet. He stood tall, mean and hard-looking in a black mackintosh and wide-brimmed hat.

And he'd killed his own brother.

A coldness settled in Alice's gut. She didn't know how he had managed to frame Uncle Hank for the murder; it was unimportant. Blood meant nothing to him. He killed his brother and intended to see his nephew, his own kin, swing for it. He spoke of contempt. Alice had never seen a man who deserved it more than Nathan Bonet.

She had a clear shot.

Pulling the trigger's easy. It's the living with it after that's hard.

Alice held back, her uncle's warning fresh in her mind. The man in her sights was family. Killing him would make her no better than
~~~

him. Could she live with his death on her hands?

Whatever she decided to do was on her. Uncle Hank was in a bad way, his lungs filled up; she could hear it. Not the same as the pox, but it sounded like it could kill him just the same. He needed to sweat the poison out – a sweat lodge. She would need help to build one.

And what of afterwards? If she were able to save Uncle Hank, what was to keep somebody else from coming for him on a cold morning when least expected? If there was a reward on his head, bounty hunters would track him down. The only way to put an end to looking over his shoulder for the rest of his life was to clear his name; the only way to do that was to bring the real killer to justice. That man was hunkered over the campfire a few yards away.

She needed Nathan Bonet alive.

The wind carried the smell of frying bacon and fresh coffee. Her stomach rolled for a taste. It preferred bacon and coffee over hardtack and water.

Alice stood and moved from the shadows.

~~~

Hank saw Alice appear at the edge of the campfire's glow and believed her a mirage.
~~~

Nothing else could explain her being there when she was back minding the ranch like he told her. The euphoria that came over him at the sight of her surprised him. He had not realized how much he missed her. She wore the brimmed wool hat he remembered, and a dark slicker that stopped below her knees.

The Winchester poked out from under it. Firelight glinted off the barrel.

Nathan stood and drew.

Hank's stomach clenched. "No!" he shouted, but the word choked on the tightness in his throat and set off another round of coughing.

No! Please, not Alice.

~~~

Alice's heart beat like a scared jackrabbit's. Her mouth went dry. She did not try to outdraw him, for it would be the last mistake she ever made. She stood stock still, held the Winchester at her side, ready. "You want him alive, I can help," she said in a voice stronger than she felt. "You shoot me, I can't help."

He squinted into the shadows. "You must be Alice."

"I am."

"Put down the rifle and come warm yourself, girl."
~~~

"The rifle stays with me."

"I got to admit, I didn't expect you to follow us. Your uncle must mean a lot to you."

"He does. Just like he means a lot to you, 'cept for different reasons."

This seemed to set him back. The air between them crackled like pond ice on a frosty morning. "How much do you know?" he asked.

"Enough."

Uncle Hank coughed. It went on for some time and sounded like it tore him up inside. He may have been trying to speak, but the words got lost.

Alice willed herself not to pay him any mind, kept her eyes on Nathan Bonet. "Ain't neither one of us gonna get what we want, you don't let me tend to him."

"Like I said, give me the rifle and you can come on in and do all the doctorin' you want."

The weight of the Winchester in her hand felt solid and real pressed against her leg. Pa gave her this rifle, showed her how to use it. Ma taught her to hunt with it. Uncle Hank told her to never let it leave her side.

She allowed a look at her uncle then, tethered like an animal, his skin too pale and his face tight with hurt. If he didn't get help soon, he would surely die.

She looked back at Nathan Bonet. The hardness in his eyes made her skin jumpy. She was a threat to him and his plans. But as long as he believed she could keep Uncle Hank from dying, he wouldn't hurt her.

That's what she told herself as she raised the Winchester from under the slicker and held it out to him.

He took it, stepped back and asked, "Got anymore shooters hiding under there?"

Alice lifted her slicker chest high. Its bunched folds pressed the knife in her bib pocket against her breastbone.

Nathan holstered his pistol. "Come warm yourself." He motioned to the fire.

Alice ignored his invitation and went to her uncle, sliding the medicine bag off her shoulder.

Nathan snatched it from her before she could blink. "What've you got there?" He pulled the bag open and looked inside. "Good God, it stinks. What is all this?"

Alice grabbed the bag back. "Nothin' you'd know how to use," she said. "I'm gonna need hot water." She turned away, not waiting for a response, and knelt at Uncle Hank's side.

He smelled of sweat and sickness.

Memories of her family dying in their beds rushed at Alice, pressed against her eyes and lodged in her throat. Helplessness welled in her. She'd tried to save them; they all died. What made her think she could save her uncle?

This isn't the same. This isn't smallpox. Help him.

She focused, saw Uncle Hank staring at her.

"What are you doing here?" he muttered.

She could see how hard it was for him to talk and keep from coughing. She knew what to give him for that. She knew how to treat fever, stomach upset, congestion. She had what she needed in her ma's medicine bag. "I'm savin' your life," she informed him.

"I told you – "

"I know what you told me," Alice snapped. "And I didn't listen. Ma said I only listen when I want to. Lucky for you, I listened when she told me how to treat sickness."

"Alice, please. Go."

"Not without you." She pulled back the blankets to loosen the rope binding his wrists.

The air stirred behind her. "He stays tied," Nathan said. He looked down at her, his face cast in shadows.

It put Alice at a disadvantage that she

didn't care for, so she stood. "He's too weak to even sit up. You afraid he's gonna *crawl* away?"

"He stays tied."

Alice decided she liked his face better when she couldn't see it all that good. And this was an argument she had no way of winning. She held her tongue.

"Water's heating on the fire," he said. "How'd you get here?"

"Got two horses tethered back in the trees." She tipped her head in their direction. "I'm gonna need my bedroll, and some things in the saddlebags."

"And another shooter, most likely. You're staying put."

"I ain't sleepin' on no dead man's blankets."

Nathan stared at her, no doubt hoping to make her nervous. She was plenty nervous, but she'd not give him the pleasure of knowing it. She held her ground and stared back.

"I'll fetch the horses," he finally said, and took up her rifle. "I don't reckon you'll run off, considering the circumstances. One of those horses Hank's white stallion?"

"It is."

"Shouldn't be hard to find in the dark."

Alice didn't take a breath until his black hat and mackintosh faded into the shadows.

~~~

The strong smell of mint wafted from the cup Alice held to his mouth. "Drink," she told him. "It'll open your lungs, help you breathe. I put ginger in it to settle your stomach."

Hank took a sip. It felt good going down. He took another, then asked, "Where is he?"

"I sent him to fetch the horses."

Fetch? Hank couldn't imagine Nathan Bonet *fetching* for anybody, especially a twelve-year-old girl. If he thought about it too hard, he'd laugh, and laughing tore him up inside. "You trust him?"

"Only as far as I can spit."

"You can't spit."

"Exactly."

Hank couldn't help himself. He'd seen Alice try to spit, remembered her indignation at getting more spittle on herself than the bug she'd been aiming at. The laugh came on too sudden to stop and triggered more coughing. Pain seized his ribcage and he coughed until tears filled his eyes.

"You've got yourself some bruised ribs, don't you."

Hank nodded, tried to answer between wracking jags.

"Don't talk. You can tell me about it once
~~~

we're outta this fix. Rest now, get your strength back."

Spent, he refused to relax until he was sure she knew what kind of danger she had put herself in. "He can't let you live."

Alice got that set look on her face Hank knew well. "I know."

Chapter 13

When Nathan returned with Penny and the stallion, Alice checked their saddlebags. Uncle Hank's hatchet, pistol, and all the ammunition were gone. *No doubt tucked under that mackintosh.* After she tended to the horses, she encouraged Uncle Hank to eat half a cold biscuit. It came back up almost as soon as it hit his stomach, doubling him over in pain.

Alice chastised herself for trying to rush things and bringing him misery. She wiped his face with a damp neckerchief, and asked, "Think you could keep a little more tea down?"

He gave a weak nod.

Once she'd gotten more ginger-laced mint tea in him, she sat close until he'd drifted to sleep. Then she joined Nathan at the campfire.

"Help yourself to some hot grub," he said,

motioning toward the skillet with his plate and spoon.

Alice offered him a biscuit. Better *he* choke on it than her uncle. He raised a brow as if surprised but took it from her. She heaped a plate with bacon and fried potatoes, and sat cross-legged by the fire. She didn't stop eating until all that remained on the plate was grease, which she mopped up with her last biscuit.

"Something to wash it down?" Nathan held the coffee pot out.

She nodded and accepted the tin cup he filled, using her coat sleeves to keep from burning her hands. All civil and polite, yet Alice felt the tension below the surface, like a snake ready to strike from under a rock.

Uncle Hank groaned, rolled over, coughed feebly before quieting again.

"You sure he's going to make it?" Nathan asked her.

No, I'm not sure at all. "Tomorrow we'll build a sweat lodge to clear his lungs."

He smirked. "We will, huh?"

"I can't build it by myself," she stated matter-of-factly, "and it's what he needs right now."

"You learn this from your ma?"

Your ma, the half-breed.

He didn't have to say it; Alice heard it in his tone. "I learned a lot of things from Ma," she said, and held his gaze long enough that his brows narrowed and he looked away.

Alice continued to watch him over the rim of her cup. The hard lines of his face danced in the light from the fire, his eyes reflecting the flames like yellow glass. Hard and unyielding. He murdered his own brother and intended to see his nephew hanged for it. What made her think she could take him to Laramie to clear her uncle's name? He was a full-grown man and she but a skinny girl.

I shoulda shot him when I had the chance.

"How far are we from Laramie?" she asked.

He looked at her sudden, his gaze brittle. "Why do you want to know?"

Alice attempted to shrug off his suspicion. "Just that it might make a difference whether Uncle Hank can survive the ride is all."

"You let me worry about that."

Alice held her tongue, took a sip of coffee. Her uncle told her true. There was no way Nathan Bonet would let her live. Neither one of them were safe. She set her empty cup down and stood. "Thanks for the grub."

~~~

She got little sleep, given her uncle's
~~~

restlessness and Nathan lying a few feet away with her Winchester tucked under his covers. The urge to sneak over and take it back once the fire died down was strong. But the odds of waking him and meeting those mean eyes in the dark kept her burrowed under her blankets.

Still, it gnawed at her.

Nathan was the first to rise come dawn. Alice heard him go off into the brush. She looked up and saw the Winchester in his hand before he disappeared behind a tree. An instant later she heard him pissing and it awakened a need of her own.

The clouds had cleared overnight and the air had a winter bite to it as she shoved her feet into her boots and dashed for the brush at the opposite end of camp. When she returned with her bladder relieved and an armload of firewood, Nathan had last night's coals kindled and was setting up to fix breakfast.

Uncle Hank moved. Alice dropped the wood beside the fire and went to him. His skin looked transparent in the light of morning. He gave a feeble cough that made his eyes water.

He's worse off.

"I gotta pee," he groaned.

Nathan rose. "Tend the potatoes," he told

her, and loosened Uncle Hank's tether from the tree root.

A thread of sick fear twisted Alice's insides as she watched Nathan support her uncle's frail body, half carrying him into the brush. He wore a stranger's clothes, the pant legs too short, yet they hung loose on him. She had to look away to keep from crying.

He can't die.

Once he'd climbed back under the blankets, Alice coaxed more mint tea into him, though it seemed a wasted effort. He turned down food and fell into a restless sleep.

Alice ate the fried potatoes and pork Nathan dished up for her only because she knew she'd need it for the work ahead. She missed fresh eggs and her uncle's sausage gravy. She missed kneading bread dough on the floured board Pa made, and the smell of biscuits baking. She missed clean clothes and the feel of Ma's quilts wrapped around her.

Anger yanked Alice from her thoughts. *Stop being a baby and feeling sorry for yourself.*

With breakfast out of the way and the coffee drained, she stood and said, "Let's get started."

Nathan grunted. "I ain't takin' orders from no girl."

"You want to keep him alive long enough to hang," Alice stated bluntly, "you'll help me. Otherwise we can just sit here and wait for him to die. You saw how weak he is."

Nathan studied her, the muscles of his jaw tight. Finally he shook his head and stood. "Let's get to it."

"We'll need large rocks," Alice said, "the size of a man's head or bigger, so they won't explode when the heat hits them." *Grandfather rocks.*

She and Nathan searched the surrounding area and found where a hillside had given way, exposing a tumble of boulders. Nathan spread out one of the dead men's slickers to roll the rocks onto. Alice leaned into the weight of the makeshift sled, matching Nathan's steps. For a man old enough to be her grandpa, he was strong and pulled his own. The work warmed them and they shed their coats.

While Nathan built a fire over the mound of rocks, Alice gathered long, flexible willow branches for the lodge frame, her ma's teachings coming back to her in bits and pieces. She showed Nathan where to dig a small pit, then together they bent the branches she'd gathered into a dome encircling the pit, lashing them in place with rawhide thongs. *Mother's womb.*

Alice silently gave thanks to the dead men for providing blankets to cover the frame. A loose flap for a door faced the mound of heating rocks. She pulled a pouch of dried tobacco leaves from the medicine bag and sprinkled it around the perimeter, a gift to the Great Spirit to bless Mother Earth.

"Waste of good tobacco, if you ask me," Nathan said.

Alice glared at him. "I didn't."

"All this," he waved a hand around as if swatting at a fly, "is injun nonsense."

"You got a better idea?"

He dropped his hand and frowned at her. "Get on with it, girl."

"Set a pot of water and a dipper alongside the rock pit. It's time."

~~~

Alice gently nudged her uncle awake. "We're going to take a sweat now," she told him.

He nodded and she helped him sit up, then braced his shoulders until his wheezing cough passed.

"We gotta get some of these clothes off you." She unbuttoned his shirt, looked at Nathan, and said, "You're going have to untie
~~~

him."

She could see he didn't much care for the idea, but he stepped in and worked the knot at Uncle Hank's wrists free. "I'll finish this," he told her. "You do whatever it is you do next."

"Leave his long johns and socks on."

Alice kept her eye on Nathan until she was sure he couldn't see her palm the folding knife from her bib pocket. She pulled off her boots and stripped down, tucked the knife inside her sock, where it would go unnoticed beneath the leg of her long underwear. Little warmth came from the noonday sun shining through the thin clouds. She wrapped a blanket around herself and collected the medicine bag.

Nathan hauled Uncle Hank to the sweat lodge. Shedding her blanket, Alice crawled in and Uncle Hank followed. He sat cross-legged next to her, shoulders slumped forward, arms folded across his middle. His tangled hair fell over his face and Alice pushed it back. The vacant look of pain on his face scared her.

"You're not afraid of catchin' what he's got?" Nathan asked, peering inside.

Alice wished she was good at spitting. She'd land a thick wad in the middle of his sneer. "My whole family died of smallpox while I watched. What do you think?"

He made no reply.

Just as well, Alice thought. She had more important things to tend to. "Bring in four of those hot rocks," she instructed. "Put them in the pit, one in each of the four directions."

Using a broad, thick slab of Douglas fir bark, Nathan carried the rocks in one at a time. When they were set in place, Alice sprinkled dried herbs over them: sage to purge negative energies, sweet grass to welcome healing spirits, cedar for purification. She remembered Ma using lungwort for little Joey's croup and sprinkled some of that over the rocks, as well.

"Now drop the flap," she said, "and leave us be 'til I give a shout for more rocks."

"Injun nonsense," he muttered, but did as told, plunging Alice and her uncle in darkness.

Alice felt for the pot of water, filled the dipper and held it out in front of her, where she knew the pit to be. "I offer these gifts to our ancestors," she said softly, "north and south, east and west, that they might guide me and cleanse my uncle of sickness." She didn't remember all the words Ma used, offered up the ones she could recall and hoped the Great Spirit forgave her shortcomings as she poured water from the dipper.

The rocks hissed. Damp, warm steam

brushed her skin, filled the air with a mix of aromas, sweet and pungent.

~~~

Hank raised his head, kept his arms wrapped around his ribcage, as he forced his shoulders back and drew in the herb-laden steam. His throat tightened. "Could I have some of that water?"

The dipper touched his lips and he drank. He coughed, waited for the pain to subside, then drank again. "Pour more of it on the rocks," he said when he'd had his fill.

The rocks hissed anew and he breathed in, deeper this time. The steam's warmth made its way to his lungs, loosening the tautness in his chest.

"Do you remember any of the prayers to the great spirits?" Alice asked.

"Mother spoke them in Arapaho," he said. "The words are gone from me."

"I wish I remembered more."

"You did well."

As the warmth in the lodge intensified, Hank felt his muscles, his entire body, ease. His mind hovered somewhere between consciousness and the dream world. He'd been eleven or twelve when he had his last sweat. Mother was trying to teach him the ways of her
~~~

people and he resisted.

"What good will knowing this do me in the white man's world?" he asked her.

"You are half *Hinono'eino*. It is your duty to carry on the traditions."

"The *Hinono'eino* are treated like animals. I want nothing to do with their traditions."

"Why must you always be angry, like *noo'uusooo'*?"

Like there is a storm coming. That was his mother's name for him: *Noo'uusooo'*. "It will protect me," he told her.

"It will make you weak, like your father. *Nonsih'ebiihii*." A drunkard.

Hank had stayed, listened to her words. He did not want to be like his father. But he remembered little of his mother's teachings, for he did not want to be like her, either. Arapaho.

The ache of regret that had become a part of him rose in his throat. "*Biixoo3e3en, Neinoo*." I love you, Mother. "*Heni'no'o3i3ecoot*." I am deeply sorry.

~~~

Alice heard her uncle groan, heard him speak Arapaho words, some she didn't recognize, and knew him to be in a dream state. She left his healing to the will of the Great Spirit.
~~~

Twice more she had Nathan bring grandfather rocks into the sweat lodge and refill the pot with water. He did as she said, but resentment and impatience burned in his eyes as the day wore on.

Chapter 14

Clouds moved in with dusk. The smell of snow hung in the air as Alice changed into dry clothes under cover of her blankets. Nathan stood with his hand on the butt of his pistol while Uncle Hank struggled into his own clothes – long johns, a gray flannel shirt, and black trousers retrieved from his bedroll. He was plenty weak, but his cough had eased some, rattled less when it did come on. Alice figured with bed rest and food, he'd be over the worst of it before long.

But his bruised ribs needed more time. He would not be able to sit a saddle until they healed. Nathan's patience would not hold out that long.

Her patience had grown short too.

When she shook free of the blankets and

stood, she realized she held Pa's folding knife concealed against the side of her leg. She considered its presence, the feel of it in her hand. No clear plan formed in her mind, just that feeling in her gut Ma told her to trust.

Once he had finished dressing, Uncle Hank eased back and took short, rapid breaths, clearly worn out by the exertion. Nathan reached for the rope tether.

"No!" Alice put as much intent in her voice as she could muster.

Nathan stopped and looked over at her, his brows lifted as though questioning an unruly child.

It fueled Alice's temper. "You ain't tyin' him to that root like a dog no more."

"You don't give the orders here, girl." Nathan straightened, faced her square. "I played along with your sweat lodge, and I will admit, it appears to have helped. Hank and I ride out in the morning."

And what about me?

"He ain't healed yet."

"Close enough." Nathan went back to binding her uncle's wrists.

"Is all this just about that scar on your face?" Alice asked hotly. "Or are you lookin' to collect a bounty, too?"

"Can't say if there's a bounty. Makes no difference, my brother's land will fetch a fine price on its own."

"So it's hate driving you." She knew she should hold her tongue, but seeing Uncle Hank tied up again made her mad. "You're so full of hate, you forgot how to be human."

"Alice, no," Uncle Hank warned, his voice forced.

She glanced over at him. *He's too weak. He won't survive the journey.* She looked back at the man standing between them.

Nathan's brows pulled into a frown that made him look downright evil. "I see it's time to tie you up too. Put a gag in that sassy mouth while I decide what to do with you."

He won't let me live.

A stillness settled Alice's angry pulse, the same stillness that came over her moments before pulling the trigger on a deer or rabbit. She would die before letting Nathan Bonet tie her up.

The folding knife felt solid and reassuring in her fist.

~~~

Hank fought to free his hands. "Leave her be!" he shouted, then doubled over coughing. Pain seared through his ribcage; he struggled
~~~

to breathe. Enraged by his helplessness, he gathered up the rope that tethered him to the tree root. His bruised body screamed. The root held.

~~~

Alice acknowledged her uncle's torment, but didn't let her gaze waver from Nathan. She held her ground as he closed the distance between them, resisted the urge to turn and run as he reached out for her.

He smirked, said, "That's a good girl. No point fighting it." His fingertips brushed her sleeve.

Alice backhanded his arm away, seized it above the elbow and yanked him hard against her, pulling him off balance. His surprised huff smelled of sour coffee. She flipped the knife open one-handed. Using his forward momentum, she drove the blade into his gut with an underhand thrust. Nathan jerked, swiped at the knife as if swatting away a stinging insect. Alice forced the blade in to its hilt. Comprehension darkened Nathan's face then. He grabbed her hand, crushed her fingers around the knife handle.

Alice pushed her weight into the hold. No different than dressing a deer, she told herself. The warmth of his blood spilled onto her skin.
~~~

Bile rose in her throat. Nathan took a faltering step back, his grip weakening.

She moved with him, kept pressure on the knife.

A gut-shot animal can live for days before dying, slow and painful. Alice would not allow that to happen. Her cry mixed with Nathan's as she forced the blade up through him until she felt it strike a rib bone. "I'm sorry," she sobbed. Only then did she push away from him, the knife still clutched in her grip.

Nathan grasped at his torn body with both hands, stared down at the blood running through his fingers. "I can't stop..." He swayed, stumbled back and landed hard on his butt.

Long seconds passed; Alice didn't breathe. She watched Nathan's futile efforts to keep his insides from spilling out. Blood soaked his trousers. She prayed he would die fast so she could turn away.

His eyes came up, met hers with a conflicted look. His face had gone pale and the scar stood out like a crimson rip down his cheek. "What have you done?"

Alice sucked in air heavy with the iron taint of blood, found voice to answer, "Pa taught me things too."

"But you're..."

Whatever he'd been going to say drowned in the blood that spilled from his mouth. His body sagged backward and his hands fell slack. He stared at the sky, expelled a gargled breath, then quieted.

Alice choked out a sob and dropped the knife. She thought she was ready for the feel of his death on her hands.

She was mistaken.

~~~

"Alice?"

Her name came to her in a whisper, like fine rain through the trees. She stared at the puddle of vomit at her feet. She didn't remember throwing up. Her gaze lifted to the man lying a short distance away. The man she had killed. Her hand was cold and sticky from it.

She looked down at the bloody knife at her feet. Pa's knife. She had used Pa's knife to take a man's life. The ground swam and she was falling to meet it.

"Alice!"

Her name, sharper this time, followed by a weak cough, caught her short of pitching forward.

Uncle Hank.

~~~

Hank saw the dazed disbelief in Alice's eyes as she came to him, knelt to untie him. In his struggle to free himself, he'd torn open the wound on his hand. His blood mixed with that of Nathan's as her shaking fingers worked at the knot.

"I'm sorry I brought this hurt on you," Hank told her.

"I have to bury him."

Hank thought of the dead men abandoned back at the cave trailhead, their bones likely picked clean and scattered by now. Leaving Nathan to the same fate seemed only fitting. "It can wait 'til daylight."

She shook her head, "He's kin," and moved away to gather rocks.

Hank made to get up and help, but a wave of coughing dropped him to his knees. Nausea rode the wake of pain through his body and he retched.

"You stay put," Alice said. "This is for me to do."

~~~

The fire had burned low. She added wood, lighting a larger area from which to gather. It took a long time, finding enough rocks, covering the body without looking too hard at it. Darkness came on. She could no longer see
~~~

beyond the reaches of the fire's glow. She stopped often to add more wood and warm her hands over the flames.

Once Alice had the body covered enough to suit her, she stood beside it for a few moments, searching for words to say. She could think of nothing kind or Christian, found no reason to thank the Great Spirit or ask him to guide the man safely into the next life.

Nor did she ask forgiveness for herself. Ma told her to never take a life without good reason. She'd had reason plenty. That didn't make it right; it was just the way of it. No amount of regret or justifying changed the facts. She had killed a man.

Nathan Bonet.

Blood kin.

She considered burying Nathan's wool sombrero with him, then thought better of it. Uncle Hank needed a hat. She set it next to him on the blanket. Nathan's coat hung from the branch where he'd put it while helping to build the sweat lodge. Alice took it down and laid it over her uncle. He had fallen into a restless sleep, interrupted often by weak attempts to cough. The sheen of fever dampened his brow.

He's a long ways from being up to riding. It worried on Alice.

Pa's knife lay where she'd dropped it. She washed it off, not allowing herself to look too close at the bits of gore floating in the water, folded it and returned it to its place in her bib pocket. When she retrieved her Winchester from Nathan's bedding, she found her uncle's Colt. Alice checked the load and laid it with the sombrero. The Winchester she carried with her to tend the horses.

They were unhappy at being tied up for such a long stretch; or maybe it was the smell of blood that unsettled them. The palomino pawed the ground and tossed his head, his mane like a white flag whipping in the night. "You're eager to be on the move, aren't you?" Alice said.

She reset their picket line to fresh grazing, gave them water and a handful of grain. Penny's keen brown eyes watched on. She blew a cloud of warm air redolent of grass at Alice's approach. Alice laid her head against the filly's neck and stroked the soft underside of her chin. Penny nudged her shoulder, melting into the attention.

The familiarity of the contact with her dear friend chipped at the ice wall Alice had put around her emotions. If she didn't feel, she didn't have to think.

"I did an awful thing," she murmured into Penny's neck, tears pressing at the backs of her eyes.

The filly tipped her head and rubbed her cheek against Alice's arm, leaned into her as if to give consolation.

The gesture splintered the last of Alice's guard. She clung to her friend and cried.

~~~

Hank opened his eyes and made out Alice squatted by the fire. It was not yet daylight. He hadn't intended to sleep, but he seemed to have little choice in his weak condition. Fever sent chills through him. He saw Nathan's coat atop him, the man's hat next to him on the blanket. And beside it was his Colt.

Alice glanced over at him, brought him a cup of tea. His hands shook as he took it from her and drank.

"You broke open that gash," she said. "I need to clean it before it festers."

She sounded distant. Hank watched her go through the motions of washing the wound, smearing green salve on it, then binding it with a clean neckerchief. Her pale skin stretched taut over her cheekbones, her eyes puffy and bloodshot. A mound of rocks in the shadows beyond the light of the fire testified to her
~~~

having done what she'd set out to do.

"Have you slept?" he asked.

She flinched, shook her head. "Are you hungry?"

"No. You should rest, Alice."

"I will." She reached into her pocket, said, "I found this sticking out from under your bedding," and held up the wooden dog figure.

It must have fallen from his shirt pocket when he changed clothes. Hank was surprised to see it in one piece. "Pete carved it," he told her.

"Has it got a name?"

"Lucky."

The shadow of a smile crossed Alice's face then was gone.

"It's yours," Hank said.

She nodded, tucked it back in her pocket. "We're gonna need all the luck we can get."

"Why is that?"

"*Benecci'.*"

Hank recognized the word, just as other words had come to him in the sweat lodge. His mother had spoken it often during Wyoming winters, standing at the window and gazing out at the white hills on a frosted morning.

It is snowing.

Chapter 15

The expression on Nathan Bonet's face as he looked upon his torn body haunted Alice's sleep. She heard his cry as she drove the blade into him. Felt his blood on her hand as it poured from him. Saw the confusion on his face as he died.

Unforgiving and relentless, the scene repeated itself each time exhaustion pulled her into unconsciousness. When dawn lightened the sky, it was a relief to shed the blankets and quiet her mind with chores.

The snow had not lasted; frost jeweled the ground and tree branches. The rocky grave stood out stark and real in the light of day. A lump lodged in Alice's throat. She turned away, kindled the fire and set a pot of coffee on to boil.

The smell of it filled the air, familiar and reassuring. Uncle Hank stirred. Without being asked, Alice helped him out of bed so he could relieve himself. His fever had broken, but he was as wobbly as a newborn foal.

"You need to eat," she said. "Build up your strength."

He made no reply, grabbed a tree branch for support, and fumbled with the buttons of his fly. Alice looked away, heard his pitiful stream. When it stopped, she helped him back to bed.

"We can't stay here," he told her, his voice raw from the cough that still tormented him.

"You're not fit to ride."

"I made it this far."

"And you were near dead when I found you," Alice reminded him sharply. "How'd you get so banged up anyway?" It was peevish of her to make it sound as if he'd done it on purpose, but the words were out and she couldn't take them back.

"Rode a landslide."

Back at the base of the cave. She remembered fearing him buried in the debris. "Did the palomino ride down with you?"

"He got clear. I'm glad you found him."

"He found me," Alice said. "He's a good

tracker. I wouldn't have located you without his help."

Uncle Hank leaned back, closed his eyes. "That's his name then. Tracker."

Alice looked over at the palomino. He met her look, blinked his white lashes at her and tossed his head. She smiled. "Tracker's a fine name."

Her uncle fell into a round of coughing painful to watch. When it played out, he asked, "You ever build a travois?"

"A horse-drawn sled." She'd seen a picture of one in Pa's books. She glanced over at the horses again. A couple of them appeared to be sturdy and even-tempered enough to pull a sled with a full-grown man on it. The prospect eased the anxiety in her stomach. "What do I do first?"

"Share that coffee."

~~~

Hank took the cup of hot, black coffee Alice handed him.

"I could make us some biscuits," she offered.

His jaw tightened at the thought of eating, but he didn't want to crush the hope he saw on her face. "That'd be fine."

The coffee tasted good, a damn sight better
~~~

than the tea he'd lost his taste for. As he watched her measure out flour, salt, and baking powder, he was reminded of all the times in the past when she'd made biscuits at home to ease her mind.

The girl had a lot to think on at the moment.

Hank's gaze drifted to the mound of rocks, put there by Alice's doing. A job for a man, not a girl. For all the times he had imagined Nathan's death, that it would come at the hands of his twelve-year-old niece never entered his thoughts. He had hoped to spare her ever looking upon the face of Nathan Bonet.

But then she took a notion to strike out on her own to find him. She had risked her life for him, and taken a life in exchange. Hank could only guess at how it weighed on her, for she did not speak of it. But he'd heard her troubled sleep, seen her eyes go distant when she paused.

It should have been me done the killing.

Alice melted lard in the fry pan, arranged rounds of dough in a single layer, and covered the pan with a lid to bake. They wouldn't be the fluffy sourdough biscuits he was use to eating at home, and there wouldn't be any of

Nan's creamy butter to spread on them, but Hank found himself anticipating their taste.

He just hoped his stomach agreed when the time came. He'd brought enough grief on the girl without getting sick on her biscuits a second time.

~~~

"Cut two poles this big around." Uncle Hank made a circle the size of her forearm with his hands. "Ten foot long."

"I don't know what ten foot looks like," Alice said, impatient over her ignorance with numbers.

"Twice as long as you are high."

She nodded, grabbed up his hatchet, and set out. Once she had the poles, she gathered half a dozen crosspieces and cut them four hands wider than a horse was broad across the shoulders. She was grateful to her uncle for explaining lengths in ways that made sense to her, and for keeping one of her biscuits down even though she'd burnt the bottoms.

"Don't know any other way to eat campfire biscuits," he told her.

Alice appreciated his effort to make her feel better, but she wasn't ready. Not yet. She could see it troubled him, her doing all the work, but there wasn't anything she could do
~~~

about that either. The weather held, but its threat weighed heavy in the thick clouds, the air sharp. She had to take her gloves off to lash the poles tight with rawhide thongs. Her hands grew cold and raw, and she had to warm them over the fire often. She did not complain, for the work occupied her thoughts.

She stopped midday to put a fresh pot of coffee on and boil a pot of salt pork and stewed tomatoes. Uncle Hank asked for another biscuit. "And I'll have some of that coffee," he said, but paled when she offered the pork and tomatoes.

Alice poured coffee, dished a plate for herself, and sat by the fire. Staring into the flames, her body at rest, her mind found its way to the thing she'd been avoiding.

I killed a man.

He deserved it, she reasoned. He killed his brother, intended to watch his nephew hang for it, and he would have killed her, his niece's daughter.

Now he's cold beneath a pile of rocks, because I put him there.

She choked back the despair that threatened to push soured salt pork up her throat. No amount of reasons made what she'd done feel right. She looked at her uncle drinking his coffee, the half-eaten biscuit in his lap. "I'm sorry," she said.

He rested his cup on his thigh. "For what?"

"You'll be a wanted man the rest of your life because of what I did."

"I'm a wanted man because of him." Uncle Hank jutted his chin toward the grave.

"Either way," she argued, "I killed the only chance you had of clearing your name. Without Nathan to confess his guilt, everybody will go on believing you're the one murdered your father."

"Find my Bowie," Uncle Hank replied.

Alice leveled a frown at him, certain the fever had muddled his mind. "What's your knife got to do with anything?"

"Nathan forged my initials on a Bowie to make it look like mine, then he stabbed his brother with it."

The depth of Nathan Bonet's heartless cruelty stunned Alice to silence. Her stomach churned at the thought of a blade the length of Uncle Hank's Bowie plunged into a person's body. She took no pleasure in knowing her grandfather's murderer had suffered the same fate at her hands. "Where's the forged knife now?" she asked.

"Locked up as evidence in Laramie,

according to Nathan."

Alice pushed to clear her thoughts, to focus on what her uncle was trying to tell her. "We find your knife and that'll prove you didn't do it." Simple. But for one thing. "It could be anywhere, most likely buried under that landslide."

"Check his gear."

Skeptical, Alice set her plate aside and went to the saddlebags beside Nathan's bedding. It didn't make sense that he'd hang onto the one thing that could prove him a lying murderer.

But there, tucked beneath a tinderbox and ammunition, she found her uncle's Bowie, along with his leg sheath. She ran a chapped finger over the initials carved in the handle, worn smooth from years of weather and use, brought the sheath to her cheek and inhaled the smell of leather and sweat. Relief pressed tears into her eyes.

After a moment, she wiped her face, went to her uncle and handed him his rig. "Keep this close."

~~~

Hank finished his biscuit and drank the second cup of coffee Alice offered him. It felt good to have the Bowie strapped to his leg
~~~

again. He'd been unable to answer Alice's question, "Why do you suppose he kept it?" He'd asked the same thing of Nathan when he saw him stow the knife in his saddlebag. "Better I know where it is," was the only response he gave. Hank figured Nathan planned to have him put the empty sheath on before they rode into Laramie, as proof that the knife in the sheriff's office did indeed belong to him. But holding onto the Bowie seemed risky.

Whatever reasons Nathan may have had for not disposing of it died with him.

The coffee helped open Hank's lungs, eased the pounding in his head. He was able to find a less painful angle to lean against the wall of the overhang but was too bruised up yet to do much else. Nathan hauling him in and out of the saddle had slowed his healing.

Alice was right, he was in no shape to be climbing onto a horse. Hank had his reservations about riding a travois, too, but he didn't see that he had much choice. There was no time to wait around for him to heal proper. Last night's brief snow had been a warning.

~~~

When Alice finished lashing the frame together, she removed the blankets and tarps from the sweat lodge. Uncle Hank told her how
~~~

to lay the bedding on the frame and tie it into place.

"Put extra at the head and shoulders," he said, "so I'm not laying flat."

Alice folded a couple blankets into the shape of pillows and secured them to the high end of the travois. She decided on the russet gelding, a quarter horse who looked to have the temperament and muscle to do the pulling.

"What do you think?" she asked the gelding, running a work-roughened hand along his neck. She stroked his muzzle, let him get comfortable with her touch and scent, then opened his mouth. He had a full set of permanent teeth, all the bottom incisors worn smooth. The two corner teeth on top had no hook and no visible groove, putting the gelding's age somewhere between eight and ten.

"You've got a lot of good years ahead of you," Alice told him.

She relied on the things Pa taught her to look for when checking a horse's health: ran her hand down each leg for lumps and hot spots, examined his feet for sores and cracks, rubbed his back and belly and rump. He stood docile, letting Alice know he was use to being tended to, treated well. She flashed on the lifeless men back at the trailhead and wondered which of them the gelding had belonged to.

Or had he been Nathan Bonet's horse?

The gelding whickered, returning Alice to the task at hand. She led him to the travois, allowed him to smell it before tying his lead to a tree. She positioned the travois behind him, careful to keep out of kicking range, should he take offense at having something in his blind spot. He turned his head from side to side, his ears swiveling with his eyes, but he showed no signs of putting up a fuss. Alice fashioned a harness to go over the horse's withers and across his chest to support the front of the frame. Then she led him around camp with the empty contraption in tow, made adjustments to eliminate any rubbing that might cause sores.

Finally satisfied, she unhitched the travois and pulled it under cover. Uncle Hank had fallen asleep. Alice was relieved that his coughing had eased enough to allow him rest. She gave the gelding a handful of grain and tethered him back with the other horses.

As the afternoon shadows lengthened, Alice sorted through gear, took stock of food, ammunition, blankets and warm clothing. Then she set about stowing it all for travel.

~~~

Early evening cast dreary shadows over the landscape. A light rain fell. Saddlebags and compact bedrolls sat beside the travois under cover of the overhang. Alice hunkered in her slicker by the fire, tending the fry pan. Exhaustion pulled at her features, weighed at her movements.

"I was afraid the bacon would go bad," she said when she saw him awake. "Figured to make it last a couple more days by frying it up."

Hank nodded, grateful the smell didn't turn his stomach. "Fine job on the travois."

"Tomorrow we'll find out how good it is." She laid the pan off to the side and helped him tend to business. Then she set him up with coffee, biscuits, and bacon, opened a can of peaches and served him a portion.

Settling next to him with her plate and cup, she asked, "How far is it to Laramie?"

"Can't say for certain." Pain and sickness had played hell with his sense of time and distance. "If we're near Soda Springs, maybe a fourteen-day ride."

"About the same as it took to get this far." Her gaze met his and Hank knew what was on her mind. "Let's end this now, go on to Laramie
~~~

and prove you're innocent, so you don't have to spend your days watching your back."

Much of his life had been spent watching his back; he'd grown accustom to it. But he saw the girl's point. There might be a bounty on his head. If he returned to the Calder ranch now, he'd be easy pickings for someone looking to cash in.

And he surely wanted to return to the ranch. He'd had a taste of the settled life; it satisfied him. "There's no guarantee a court will believe I'm innocent. Are you prepared for that?"

"No." She gave him a determined scowl. "I'm prepared for the truth to be known."

The last time Hank saw Laramie, it was a lawless town at the end of the tracks. He had no idea what they'd be riding into. He'd just as soon keep his niece clear of any more unpleasantness, but that card had already been dealt.

Alice was right; best to see this thing through. "How's our grub stock?"

"It'll stretch, if we're careful." She leaned close and whispered, "One of the men had a sack of hard candy hid in his bedroll."

For a brief moment, she looked like any young girl with a sweet tooth. It made Hank smile.

They had a lot of country to cover; a lot of things could go wrong before they reached Laramie. If they made it in one piece, it was likely he'd end up in jail. He may even be hung, as Nathan had hoped. Either way, Alice would be forced to return to Oregon on her own.

She'd need a cache.

"Bring me my saddlebags," he told her.

~~~

Alice watched her uncle remove the contents from one of the saddlebags she had so carefully packed earlier. Then he reached in and pulled the underside of the bag free. "A false bottom," she whispered, surprised she had missed it.

"When you're on the trail alone, it pays to have a secret hidey-hole." He withdrew a handful of paper money. "There's a hundred dollars here, enough to restock supplies once we reach Laramic. I wanted you to know about it, should something happen to me."

Annoyance fueled by fear swept through Alice. "Ain't nothin' gonna happen to you. I won't let it."

"I'm counting on that."
~~~

Chapter 16

By daybreak, Alice already had a fire going and was tending to the horses. Impatient to do his share, Hank attempted to get his legs under him, but they lacked the strength. He fell back in pain – a pain that ran deep in his chest yet. "Damn it," he muttered.

"You need to pee?" Alice asked, starting toward him.

"No, I don't need to pee!"

She stopped in her tracks, a stricken look on her face.

Hank sighed and hung his head. "I'm sorry, Alice."

"It's alright."

"No, it's not," he replied, irritated with himself. "I should be helping, not lying here like dead weight."

She snickered.

"What's so amusing?"

"Ma used to say Pa squalled worse 'an us kids when he was sick. She threatened to make him sleep in the barn."

"I already do that," he grumbled, then chuckled at how she'd turned his impatience into something to joke about. It set off the coughing and he clutched his chest. "Don't make me laugh."

"At least you remember how." She gave him a lopsided smile before turning away. "I'll get us something to eat."

~~~

After breakfast, Alice strapped bedrolls and saddlebags in place, then harnessed the travois to the russet gelding. She'd lead the gelding and Tracker; the other four horses she tied in a string behind Penny.

"We'd make better time turning them loose," Uncle Hank said.

"No," Alice replied firmly. "They ought to be returned to their owners' next of kin."

"That makes the dun mine then."

Nathan's horse. Laying claim to it was the closest her uncle had come to acknowledging the man as family. Alice chose not to make mention of it, given the sourness in his voice.
~~~

The dun looked to be healthy, well-tended. It appeared Nathan Bonet had treated his horse better than he'd treated his own kind, no doubt aware it could mean the difference between survival and death.

But treating his horse well had not saved him.

Alice drew an unsteady breath. She'd had more troublesome dreams, slept little. Would her thoughts ever be her own again?

"Let's get you on the travois," she told her uncle.

~~~

Hank felt every rock and twig and root the apparatus bounced over; and there were many. He was warm and dry in Nathan's woolen coat and black mackintosh. Likewise Nathan's hat, made of fine fur, fit well, had a wide brim, and protected his head. Alice had bundled him like a newborn babe against the bitter cold. The extra padding at his shoulders allowed him to sit up and relieve the pull on his bruised body.

But nothing could be done to smooth the trail that weaved through the trees.

Riding the travois put Hank abreast of the horse string. He had not argued with Alice's decision to return them to their owners' families. It was the right thing to do. It
~~~

wouldn't bring their men home, but a good horse, like Mateo's charcoal gelding, could well mean survival for a family. Hank would do nothing to quell Alice's sensibilities, for those sensibilities separated her from others less compassionate – others like Nathan Bonet.

And himself.

The travois jolted and Hank stifled a grunt. He pulled the hat low over his face and attempted to shut out his discomfort.

~~~

The trail Alice followed led east, to a low pass in the mountains. Fresh snow dusted the rounded summits. She pressed to put distance on the gravesite camp, hoping to out-ride the images that plagued her there. Yet sitting a saddle gave her little else to do but reflect, and her thoughts continued to ambush her.

By midday, a light, cold rain had begun to fall, and the gap in the mountains opened onto a lush valley. A river flowing from another band of hills to the north meandered through the abundant grasses. Steam rose from the surface of a spring that fed into the river. Alice dismounted, pulled off a glove and was surprised to find the stream's water warm to the touch.

Keen to scrub the stink of death from her
~~~

skin, she announced, "We'll hold up here a bit."

Rain had pooled in the meadow, providing sufficient fresh water for the horses. Once Alice had a tarp strung up, she helped Uncle Hank to sit under its shelter. He looked worn out, and Alice worried she had pushed too hard.

"I'll get us a fire," she said.

Wood was abundant at the edge of the timber, and she soon had a blaze to lend warmth. The light patter of the rain on the tarp, and the snap and pop of the fire, eased Alice's tight back and neck. A brief peace settled in her.

"If we continue east," Uncle Hank said, "we should hit Soda Springs before long."

"Ma talked of such a place. She said they washed and bathed in hot mineral water that bubbled and tasted like soda." At the time, Alice had been sure Ma made up the stories to coax her and little Joey to sleep at night. "Do people live there?" she asked.

"I believe so."

"If there's a price on your head, it's best we avoid settlements." As she said it, Alice realized that had probably been Nathan Bonet's intent.

"Agreed," Uncle Hank said.

Perturbed that Nathan Bonet had once

again intruded on her thoughts, Alice stated, "Strip to your long johns. We're goin' swimming."

"Don't know about the swimming part," Uncle Hank remarked, and pushed the slicker from his shoulders.

Reminded of her grandmother's death, Alice asked, "Do you know how to swim, Uncle?"

"Well enough to keep my head above water." He reached for a boot and grimaced. While Alice helped with his boots, she told him about finding Grandma Ela's marker hidden in the brush along the Snake River. "Did you see it when you came through?"

"I regret I did not."

"I'll point it out when we go back that way."

Uncle Hank fell quiet, and she glanced up. He averted his gaze. *He doesn't believe he's coming back.* Alice tried not to let it annoy her.

"Annie wrote that your pa taught you to swim," he said.

"Like a fish. He didn't want to chance us kids meeting the same fate as our grandma." She gave her head a sad shake. "Pa said it wouldn't have mattered if she knew how to swim that day, though. The water was too swift."

"Won't be a problem here." Uncle Hank pointed his chin at the hot spring. The water was no deeper than a wash tub.

"Once you're healed, I'll give you lessons," Alice promised, and helped him to the water's edge.

~~~

Hank lowered himself into the warm, rippling current, sighed in relief as he became buoyant. He drifted to a natural pool behind a low, smooth rock to relax and let the hot spring water soothe his sore body. The tightness in his chest loosened, and his breathing eased. He rinsed caked mud from his scalp, then rested his head back on the rock, closed his eyes, and took pleasure in the patter of cool rain on his face. Wordsworth's poem of wandering like a cloud came to mind, golden daffodils tossing their heads along the shore.

"You got a bar of soap hid in those saddlebags?" Alice called.

Hank smiled at the interruption to his musing. "Nope."

She'd found a spot of her own upstream a short ways and was doing what she could to scrub herself through her long underwear. Her hair, freed from its braids, floated around her shoulders like a copper cape. She shot him a
~~~

smile that made her eyes sparkle.

It was a welcome sight after all she'd been through. Hank stowed the image in his heart, to call on should troubled times come between them. It concerned him that she continued to talk of their return to Oregon together; he did not share her optimism.

Alice's smile wavered. "A cloud just passed over your face," she said. "Do you need to get out?"

Hank regretted dampening her fragile mood. He cupped his hands together and shot a spout of water in her direction. "I'm not a prune yet."

She gave a light laugh and returned to bathing.

~~~

Alice added wood to the fire and put coffee on to heat. She worked quickly, her chilled skin covered with goose bumps. Reluctant to dress in clothes that smelled from days of horse and sweat, she put her slicker on over her wet underwear and used the warmth of the fire and her own body heat to dry out.

Uncle Hank had asked her to find him a walking stick so he could get around without hanging onto her so much. He propped himself near the fire, a slicker over his wet long
~~~

johns, and gazed into the flames like he had a lot on his mind.

It was good to see him standing, breathing easier. His long johns clung to his wasted body, but Alice knew he'd fill out soon enough, now that he was eating better.

She also knew the cause of his faraway look, but refused to pay it mind. Once he proved to the judge that there was no way he could have killed his father, they'd be back on Calder Ranch, sleeping in warm beds and eating Nan's fresh-churned butter on biscuits that weren't burnt.

She shivered and moved closer to the fire's heat. "Let's wait 'til morning to light out," she said. "We both need a clean change of clothes."

~~~

Hank welcomed any excuse to postpone climbing aboard the travois again. Standing on his own was improvement, but he weakened too easy and knew he was still in no condition to straddle a horse. He and Alice ate a cold meal of dried apples, biscuits and bacon, finished off the coffee, then she went to the stream's edge to wash out their clothes.

A short while later, Alice had strung lines under cover of the tarp, and their shelter looked like a laundry. Her busyness was more
~~~

than Hank could stand. "If you'll fetch some water," he said, "I'll cook up a deer meat stew for supper." He figured he could manage that much, at least.

She smiled. "You got a deal."

~~~

The man with the scarred face wrapped a rope around Uncle Hank's neck. Alice tried to scream, but she couldn't open her mouth. The man grinned at her as he cinched the rope tight. Her uncle's face turned purple. No! She couldn't push the sound past her lips. Helpless, she watched the man choke Uncle Hank to death.

No! No!

"Alice?"

She opened her eyes, blinked in confusion at the flicker of firelight on the tarp overhead. Her heart raced. Slowly, she slanted her gaze to the side, afraid of what she'd see.

Uncle Hank was sitting up, looking at her. *Alive.*

"You alright?" he asked softly.

Alice pressed her fingers to her lips, realized she could open them after all. A dream. That's all it was. A really bad dream. "He was killing you," she said. "I couldn't do anything to stop him."

But she *did* stop him. And it was no dream.
~~~

In real life, she had killed the man with the scar.

Frustrated, she asked, "Does it ever get any easier? Living with it?"

Uncle Hank drew in a long, slow breath. "It will in time. But it'll always be a part of you."

It wasn't the answer she wanted, but it was one she thought she understood. "This is what you tried to warn me about, isn't it, the day I wanted to shoot Pressfield."

"No, Alice." There was sorrow in the look he gave her. "You wanted revenge. That's not the same as killing to survive."

Never take a life without good reason. Alice studied her uncle in the glimmer of light from the dying fire. He'd talked of survival in a white man's world; she knew he had killed to defend himself at the cave trailhead. How many deaths did he carry on his conscience? "Did you ever take a life out of revenge?" she asked.

He turned away, stared into the firelight without answering. Alice could see her question troubled him, and she wished she had not asked it. She was about to apologize, when he broke his silence.

"It happened ten years ago, in Saltillo, Mexico," he said. "That's where I met Ruth

Flores. She was selling the silver jewelry her father had crafted in the market." His voice softened. "I don't know what she saw in me, but we enjoyed each other's company."

Alice raised up on an elbow, eager to know more about this woman he had never mentioned until now. "Was she pretty?"

"Beautiful," he answered, and gave Alice a smile. "She had long black hair to her waist. Gentle hands. Her dark eyes shined when she laughed and flashed lightning bolts when she was angry."

"Did you ever make her angry?"

He grunted. "All the time. But she agreed to marry me just the same. Her parents did not approve, particularly her father. I was a gringo half-breed, a drifter without a stable trade, no property." He shrugged and said, "It didn't matter. We were in love." His sadness returned, took on a hard edge. "Two days after we married, she was killed."

Alice's breath caught. "I'm sorry, Uncle."

"We were in a hotel room on the second floor. It was a warm evening and we had the window open. A man came out of the *cantina* across the street, drunk, shouting something about being cheated. He fired off a wild shot that came through the window and killed Ruth almost instantly."

Tears filled Alice's eyes.

"I caught the man, dragged him up to the room and showed him what he'd done. He begged for mercy." Uncle Hank paused. "I shot him anyway."

Alice realized it still troubled him, deeply, after all this time. He wore the regret of it on his face. It didn't matter that he'd been avenging the death of the woman he loved. He could not forgive himself for taking a life when his own had not been in danger.

That's what he was protecting me from.

"Thank you for telling me, Uncle."

~~~

Alice seemed to sleep better after their talk. Hank slept not at all. He saw the joy in Ruth's eyes moments before a bullet turned it to confusion. Felt the warmth ebb from her body. Relived the grief and rage that consumed him. Smelled the rancid alcohol on her killer's breath, his urine as he pissed himself. *¡Por favor, ten compasion! ¡Ten compasion, señor!*

The deafening repercussion.
~~~

Chapter 17

By morning the rain stopped and the sun made a weak attempt to burn through the clouds. Alice and her uncle finished the stew and biscuits, drank a pot of coffee, then pulled up camp and headed east.

They had not gone far when they reached a knoll that looked down on a cluster of buildings at the bend of a river. Soda Springs. The grass-covered bottom stretched several miles across, the mountains south of the settlement thick with pine timber. Ready firewood, fresh water, plentiful grazing: it was easy for Alice to see why emigrants moving west, like her ma and pa, had chosen to linger. Some decided to stay and stake a claim.

Alice skirted wide of the settlement. On the east bank of the river, a small cone formation puffed and spewed milky water. A split in the rocks hissed pungent gas into the cold air.

"Steamboat Spring," Uncle Hank called up to her from the travois.

Alice had never seen the likes. She watched mesmerized for long minutes before nudging Penny to move on.

The trail hugged the river as it curved south, then unfolded east through a broad valley with scattered groves of leafless aspen poking bony fingers at a gray sky. Ahead of them was a steep ridge of mountains, the uppermost peaks dusted with snow. Alice slowed their pace as they began to climb, for the horses made hard work of it in the thinning air. The weather remained dry but sharp. Patches of ice clung to the shadows of pine and fir.

They nooned on a grassy flat. A small herd of elk grazed along the edge of a creek below. Ahead, another ridge of mountains waited.

"We'll be in Wyoming once we're on the other side," Uncle Hank said.

They set up camp beside the creek that night. The elk had moved on.

The going was slower the next day, the trail steeper. They stopped often to rest the horses.

The country through which they traveled was isolated and beautiful, the surrounding peaks humbling. Though little used since the railroad went in farther south, the ruts of wagon wheels, packed hard beneath the footsteps of thousands of emigrants and gold miners heading west, left a permanent scar across the land easy to follow.

Two more ridges, traversed over as many days, gave Alice time to think about the things Uncle Hank had told her. He had loved; he had married. Then it was cruelly taken from him. She pondered on the different ways people handled such loss. When Mr. Trevor's heart gave out on him, Nan had kept her pain inside, to be strong for her boys, Ma said. Alice had looked for somebody to blame when her family died: the strangers who rode into Baker City, their faces covered with the rash, Doctor Leonard for not knowing how to treat them, herself for being so powerless.

Uncle Hank's grief sought justice.

Did that make him a bad man? Not to Alice's mind. She was learning that grief sometimes made a person do things they knew weren't right.

It's the living with it after that's hard.

Her uncle had a conscience. That's what

separated him from men like Nathan Bonet, men who killed for greed, or because it made them feel in control.

She thought back on the day of the race in Baker City. Uncle Hank had been prepared to kill the man who tried to hurt her. If she hadn't stopped him to get her own lick in, he would have choked the man to death. If that made him a bad person, then the same could be said for her. She'd killed Nathan Bonet to protect her uncle. And herself. She wished there'd been another choice, but he left her none. Her conscience had settled with that fact the day she buried him.

Then why did it continue to trouble her sleep?

Uncle Hank said it would get easier in time. She believed him. She'd never forget, did not *want* to forget, but she wouldn't feel guilt for what she'd done either.

Alice sighed, breathed in the striking, snow-capped mountains. The more she tried to make sense of humankind, the more she realized how impossible the task. Easier to understand nature, the coming and going of the seasons, the behavior of birds and insects, deer and jackrabbits.

Uncle Hank's health continued to improve,

though not nearly fast enough to suit him. He was prickly as a dried out pine cone over his weakness.

At the end of the fourth day, they stopped a few miles shy of Green River to set up camp. Uncle Hank rolled off the travois, took up his walking stick, and stated, "I've had my fill of traveling over every root and stone in Wyoming on my back."

Alice paused gathering wood for the fire and eyed him leaning on his stick, his legs unsteady beneath him. "You plan to walk?"

His gaze cut to Tracker. "I plan to ride."

"You're not strong enough yet."

"I can sit a saddle."

"You're gonna make yourself sick again with your stubbornness."

"You're one to talk about being stubborn."

Alice shrugged. "If you can get on Tracker, you can ride. I ain't helpin'."

"I didn't ask for your help."

"Prickly as a dried out pine cone," Alice muttered, and went back to building a fire.

~~~

Over supper that evening, Hank said, "Once we've crossed Green River, there's forty miles of desert known as Sublette's Cutoff. We'll need to carry all the water we can. Won't
~~~

be much for the horses to eat, but they'll get by as long as we can keep them watered. How's the grub holding up?"

"The last of the meat turned bad," Alice said. "I'll go hunting in the morning."

Hank nodded. "I'll build a jerking rack from the travois. The dried meat will last longer."

"You really intend to ride tomorrow?"

"I do."Hank chuckled. "You really think I'm prickly as a pine cone?"

Alice choked on her coffee and her face turned red.

~~~

At first light, Hank watched Alice take up her Winchester and slip from camp. He rousted himself out of bed, did a passable job of stoking the fire, and set the pot of beans that had been soaking overnight on to boil. Then he went to work on a jerking rack.

He cut the two longest poles of the travois above the last crossmember and lashed them to the rest of the frame as support legs. It took but one swing of the hatchet to remind him of his injuries. He grit his teeth, determined to work through it. Alice had been right to accuse him of stubbornness. Must be a Bonet trait, he thought.
~~~

He heard a shot, had coffee ready when Alice dragged a nice little mule deer into camp. The fixed set of her jaw and the hollow look in her eyes told him killing it had not come easy. Her dreams continued to wake him with muffled whimpers and crying out. Her suffering pained him worse than his bruised body.

"I'll dress that," he told her once she had the deer strung up.

"No." Sharp, heated. With her back to him, she added softly, "I have to."

Hank did not argue, knowing she needed to work through it her own way. He kept an eye on her while he scattered the fire and set the jerking rack in place. She hesitated often, stifled sobs as she gutted the animal, then skinned it. Once done, she let him help her cut the meat from the carcass to hang over the cross members of the rack. Hank laid damp boughs atop the fire for smoke.

Alice said little as they ate and finished off the coffee. After their plates were wiped down, she carried the canteens to the water's edge, filled them, lingered there a time. When she returned to camp, Hank took heart at the calm in her eyes, as though she'd made peace with her troubled thoughts.

By late afternoon, the heat and smoke of the low fire had dried the deer strips into jerky that would last for several months.

"We'll leave before dawn," Hank said, "to give us more daylight crossing the desert."

"It'll give you more time to get on that horse of yours, too," Alice commented, slanting him a crooked smile.

Hank grunted and returned her smile.

~~~

Two hours before dawn, they ate a cold breakfast and packed their gear. Alice was thankful the Great Spirit listened to her prayer yesterday and allowed her a restful sleep. Gutting the mule deer had been difficult.

She watched her uncle hobble over to Tracker, take up the reins and guide him alongside a low rock. He spoke softly to the horse as he stepped up, using the cantle and saddle horn for support. Alice could not make out the words, but Tracker seemed to understand.

Uncle Hank paused as though to catch his breath, then he rubbed behind Tracker's girth, level with the horse's elbow. Tracker went into a gentle left bend that brought the saddle and stirrup lower. Taking the reins and a handful of mane in one hand, the saddle horn in the other,
~~~

her uncle put his foot in the stirrup and pushed up into the saddle. He settled in, leaned forward and coughed a spell from the effort.

Tracker shifted for balance and waited. Once his rider had recovered, he received a gentle touch and more soft words. It was obvious the stallion and its rider had done this before.

Alice could have accused her uncle of tricking her, but he looked so fine atop that palomino stallion, she let it pass. In spite of all she had learned about him, she recognized there was much she still didn't know.

And he would tell her in his own time.

Uncle Hank looked over at her standing beside Penny. Alice mounted up.

~~~

In spite of Tracker's easy step, pain throbbed in Hank's chest. He was not fit to ride, but he tightened his jaw and said nothing. The surprise on Alice's face when she saw the palomino bend low for him made the discomfort worth it. Walter Smith, the old horse wrangler he'd worked for in Nevada, taught him that trick. Hank and the palomino had made use of it on more than one occasion.

A hard frost coated the landscape. When they reached Names Hill – a steep limestone
~~~

cliff where emigrants carved their names after crossing Green River – Alice dismounted, hoping to find Anne and Joseph Calder, but the light was too poor.

The ferry took them to the other side of the river. Dawn was but a thin splinter on the horizon. Hank and Alice traveled a barren, white plain of withered sage and greasewood, into the milky haze of sunrise. Slowly, the morning frost melted, but there was little welcome in the dull gray sky. They pulled their neckerchiefs up against the fine sand that found its way into their noses and eyes, coated their clothing and gear. The horses blew the dust from their nostrils often.

Once, a jackrabbit bounded from behind a sage and into the cover of another, no other sighting of man or beast to be seen.

The day grew long. They made better time without the travois in tow, stopped often to stretch tight muscles, chew on a strip of jerky, water the horses. Hank was grateful for Alice's help getting back in the saddle.

Night fell and so did the temperature. Alice built a small fire of sage to boil coffee. They ate more jerky, some dried fruit, sucked on hard candy. Possessing no desire to linger in such an inhospitable place, they pressed on.

Sometime before midnight, they reached the deep draw of Little Sandy Creek. Dropping south a short distance, they came upon a level spot to set up camp. The horses slaked their thirst and tore at what grass was available. It was bitter cold and Alice gathered willow for a fire.

Hank felt the cold deep in his bones. It rankled him to be of so little help, but truth be told, he should not have pushed getting in the saddle. Several times throughout the day, he'd struggled to stay conscious. His head drummed from the effort.

Ice rimmed the bank of the creek by morning. The only thing for it was to keep moving. After a hot meal and coffee, they pulled up camp, crossed Little Sandy and another twelve miles of barren land, before beginning the climb to South Pass, in the Wind River Mountains.

<center>~~~</center>

Retracing the route her ma and pa had taken west brought a closeness to them Alice embraced, the stories they told her and little Joey replaying in her head and in her heart. South Pass was a broad saddle of prairie and sagebrush that crossed the Continental Divide at 8,000 feet elevation. And just like Pa said, the

Sweetwater River flowed east instead of west, its water clear and fresh from the mountains that fed it.

She and Uncle Hank crossed the river no less than nine times in the seventy-five miles to Split Rock. They saw the rock's gunsight notch a good day's ride before they reached it.

The notch was still visible two days later, when she and her uncle made Devil's Gate, where the Sweetwater had carved a deep cleft, too narrow for a wagon to pass, in the granite mountain. The river rushed through the channel, roaring over huge rock fragments lying in its course. The wind blew cold and harsh.

"When Grandma Ela came through here with Ma and Pa, she told a story of how the cleft was made," Alice said. "Do you know of it?"

"I do not."

"A giant beast with enormous tusks once roamed this valley and kept the Shoshone and Arapaho people from hunting here. One day, the hunters decided to kill the beast. They shot it with many arrows. Angered, the beast tore a huge opening in the mountainside with its tusks and escaped, never to be seen again."

Uncle Hank studied the opening a

moment, nodded and said, "It's a good story."

~~~

They set up camp at Independence Rock, a granite hump Hank thought looked like a giant turtle shell on the grassy plain.

"If travelers heading to California could reach it by the Fourth of July," Alice explained, "they had a better chance of crossing the Sierra Nevada Mountains, a thousand miles west of here, before snowfall."

Hank had seen the Sierra Nevada in winter and knew well the dangers.

Independence Rock bore the hieroglyphics of Indian warriors and pioneers alike. Once Alice had a fire going, she set out to look for her ma and pa's names in the remaining daylight. Hank stayed in camp to prepare supper. After nearly a week of riding, he had regained some of his strength but still tired easily.

Devil's Gate was a dark silhouette ten miles back. His mother's Arapaho legend about the notched mountain tugged at the part of him that was of her blood. *Hinono'eino.* Alice's knowledge of their traditions and tales had him wanting to know more. And the stories she shared at each landmark along the trail served to fill in the blanks of his sister's life.
~~~

A short time later, Alice returned to camp, her discontent clear. She took a seat next to the fire, and Hank handed her a plate of food. "Didn't hurt to try," he told her.

She shrugged. "No matter. I know they came this way. Ma said they missed the Fourth of July by two days, but they had a picnic and sang songs anyhow."

"You're fortunate to have those memories." Hank poured them each a cup of coffee and sat with her to eat.

"Do you have favorite memories of Ma, from when you were kids?" she asked.

Her question made him pause; he realized he'd allowed bitterness toward his father to overshadow the pleasant moments he'd shared with his sister. "There was a place down by the river where we'd go in the summer," he said. "We'd catch frogs and skip rocks. The long branch of a tree close to the bank reached out over an elbow of the river that created a shallow pool. On hot days, Annie and I would crawl out on that branch and let go. We'd splash around in the water awhile, then lie in the tall grass to dry off." He remembered the feel of river algae on his skin, the smell of pitch from the tree branch.

"I'd like to see it," Alice said, "the place

where you and Ma played."

"I'd like to show it to you," Hank replied truthfully. "We'll stop there before riding into Laramie."

~~~

Two days east of Independence Rock, Hank and Alice crossed the North Platte River and headed south along Little Medicine Bow, through a broad basin said to have been traversed by Cheyenne and Northern Arapaho on their way to winter at the Wind River Indian Reservation – some time after the slaughter of their people at Sand Creek, Colorado. While battles between blue and gray were fought in Eastern states, US cavalry murdered Indians on the Western plains.

Hank had spent his life drifting, distancing himself from his Indian blood, but hearing of their fate had rested uneasy on his heart. Women and children and old men butchered. It was a story he did not wish to share with Alice, though he suspected she'd heard of it from Annie. He did not think his sister one to shelter her daughter from the brutality. To do so would leave her vulnerable.
~~~

Chapter 18

The cabin where her ma and Uncle Hank had grown up didn't look like much, Alice thought with disappointment. She wasn't sure what she'd expected, but the weathered shack before her wasn't it. She and Uncle Hank had followed Little Medicine Bow River for three days to reach the Bonet homestead, located in a swath of grassland at the base of the Laramie Mountains. The closer they'd gotten, the quieter her uncle had become. Alice could only guess at the conflicted thoughts going through his head.

She made for the porch steps while her uncle pumped water into the trough for the horses. The door was shut but not latched; she pushed it open, and the rusted hinges groaned.

The draft that followed the door inside

stirred a haze of dust. Cobwebs hung from a shelf and its haphazard stack of battered tinware above the sink. A table and single chair off to one side, a cast iron cook pot and a meager stack of firewood on the hearth, a blackened poker propped against it: all that remained of the family who had once called this home.

Alice stood at the center of the room and tried to imagine her ma as a little girl playing here, eating here. But all she saw, all she felt, was emptiness.

There was a tattered blanket over a doorway in the corner. She started toward it.

"Don't."

Uncle Hank's harsh command from behind made her jump. He stood just outside the door of the cabin, as though reluctant to enter. The concerned look on his face drew her gaze back to the room. Sudden awareness chilled her.

Grandfather was murdered in there.

Her uncle moved past her, blocked her view as he pushed aside the blanket. He stood that way for long seconds, unmoving. Finally his shoulders relaxed and he stepped aside. "Alright," he said, holding the blanket back so she could see for herself.

Alice slid by him and into the room. It was

stuffy, smelled of mildew. Threadbare yellow curtains cast a broken pattern of light across a thin mattress void of bedding. Alice guessed the blankets had been used to carry Thomas Bonet's body out to be buried – as they'd done with little Joey, Ma, and then Pa. She wondered if the mattress had been turned to hide a blood stain. Her familiarity with the rituals of death left a cold hollowness in her.

A scrap of paper caught between the wall and a leg of the bed drew Alice's attention. She went to it, pulled it free. It was the faded photograph of a pretty, young Indian woman wearing a beaded leather dress and holding a bunch of wild bluebonnets. Alice saw Ma's smile and Uncle Hank's sadness in the young woman's face. "Is this Grandmother?" she asked softly.

Uncle Hank's hand shook as he reached for the photograph. "Father had it taken the day they were married."

Alice thought she understood the tightness in her uncle's voice. She had no pictures to remind her of her family. To see their faces again –

Uncle Hank held the photograph out for her to take. "Keep it safe."

"But – "

"Please. It's yours now."

Grateful to have an image to put with the stories of her grandmother, Alice's eyes teared up. "Thank you."

"I'll get wood for a fire," Uncle Hank said and turned away.

~~~

Hank walked out of the cabin and down the steps. He didn't stop walking until he reached the barn, then was behind it, where he could take deep gulps of air without drawing Alice's attention. Returning to this place had been a mistake, the memories too strong. He'd believed time would numb the hurt, but it had not. The pain of his father's blows, the anger, the disgrace. Annie's tears.

Seeing his mother's face again, a face that had become fuzzy in his mind, reminded him of the last time he'd seen her. His father had come home drunk, belligerent, mean. He'd taken a swing at Hank, and for the first time, Hank struck back. Enraged, his father beat him, then staggered to bed. Annie cried on her pallet in the corner.

Mother held cold compresses to his battered face. "You must go," she whispered. "Leave this place, tonight. If you do not, he will kill you."
~~~

"Not if I kill him first," Hank said, keeping his voice low as well. He did not wish to cause his little sister more anguish with his threat.

"You are not strong enough," his mother told him harshly.

"I will be."

"Then what? If you succeed, they will hang you. And without my white husband, I will be sent to the reservation. Do you want your sister to see you die and to be taken from her home?"

"I can't leave you and Annie unprotected."

His mother's chin came up, the look in her eyes uncompromising. "I will watch after my daughter's safety," she said. "It is my son's future I worry over. There is no life for you here."

Knowing she spoke the truth, Hank left that night after Annie fell asleep. His mother said it would be safer for his sister if she didn't know. Only one other person knew the truth behind his leaving: Mateo Blake. Hank had paid him a visit on his way out of town. It was not the first time his friend had seen his face bruised and swollen. Hank made him swear to keep an eye on his mother and little sister, told him he'd find a way to let him know where he was so they could write. He left with the certainty that he'd return some day – when he was older, wiser, stronger.

If he had, it would not have been Nathan Bonet's hand that killed his father. He'd have done it himself, without remorse.

And everything his mother had warned him of would come to be. Then, just as now, he'd be hanged.

His life had come full circle. In spite of the years he'd stayed away, hoping to keep the ones he loved safe, he had not escaped his fate. Only this time, instead of Mother and Annie's future to worry about, there was Alice's to think of.

Hank went to the woodpile, gathered an armload, and turned back toward the cabin. A thin ribbon of smoke rose from the chimney. A warm memory entered his thoughts, of his mother cooking rabbit stew, adding mint from the patch that grew wild out back. He'd forgotten how beautiful she was. He clung to that memory, held it close to his heart, as he made his way to the cabin.

~~~

Alice glanced up at the sound of her uncle's return. She did not question the time it took him to gather an armload of wood. The unsettled look in his eyes said enough. She respected what he was going through; death of family went deep, no matter the circumstances.
~~~

This place brought him face to face with it.

She added more wood to the fire and stood. "Once we've tended to the horses, I'll fix us some biscuits and gravy."

His eyes softened, focused on her. "I'd like that."

A section of roof at the back of the barn had collapsed, but the front appeared sound. She and Uncle Hank stripped gear from the horses and allowed them to roll in the hay-littered dirt of the barn floor before putting them in stalls and giving them water and feed. They worked together quietly. It was good to see her uncle moving with more ease.

She found the book of Wordsworth in his saddlebag, pulled it out and placed her grandmother's picture between its pages. *Was Grandfather holding the picture to him when he died?* Alice wanted to believe so.

Uncle Hank stood gazing at the hay loft and said, "Annie liked to hide up there and throw hay down on me. She always gave herself away with her giggles."

It pleased Alice that he had happy memories to balance the hard ones. She hoped, in time, she'd be able to hear little Joey's laughter again. She wanted to remember her brother, and Ma and Pa, as they'd been before sickness robbed them of joy.

Once the horses had been tended to, Uncle Hank took her to the river and showed her the pool where he and her ma used to splash in the water. The tree branch they'd drop from was still there. Seeing it made him smile.

~~~

Night settled and crickets sang outside the door of the cabin. Alice and her uncle sat on the hearth, eating the biscuits and gravy she'd promised.

"We'll bed down here tonight," Uncle Hank said, "wash up, and start for town in the morning."

"By this time tomorrow, your name'll be cleared and we'll be on our way home," Alice replied.

"There will be a trial. If they find me guilty —"

"They won't," Alice insisted. "You didn't kill your father."

"A judge may see different," her uncle said. "Even if I'm cleared of Thomas Bonet's murder, I killed three of the men those horses out there belonged to."

The food in Alice's stomach roiled, her taste for it gone. She set her plate down. "And I killed Nathan Bonet."
~~~

Uncle Hank gave her a sharp look. "Tell no one that."

"I ain't gonna hide from what I did."

"I mean it, Alice. If they ask you – "

"I'm no liar."

"No, you are not. But I won't have you put on trial for something that needed doing."

Just as shooting the men who'd hunted him needed doing. But Alice didn't want to argue with her uncle. What he said was true. A judge may not take kindly to all the killing, no matter how justified. What if the judge had been friends with one or more of the dead men? What if he had been a friend to Nathan Bonet?

Alice met her uncle's dark eyes, saw his concern for her, found strength from it. She hadn't traveled all this way only to return home without him. And she refused to let him take the blame for something she did. "We'll know more tomorrow," she said, and collected their dirty plates.

~~~

The town sat on the bank of the Laramie River, nestled in a valley between two mountain ranges. The last time Hank saw it, it was comprised of tent houses and log buildings thrown up in anticipation of the
~~~

transcontinental railroad. Plans were being made to lay tracks across the Laramie Plains, in what was Dakota Territory. Thugs and gamblers served as town officials and judges. The U.S. Army constructed Fort Sanders a few miles north of town to protect the Overland Stage and railroad surveyors.

Now the Union Pacific railroad line bordered the city of Laramie and crossed the river on its way to Utah Territory. A brick-front business district stretched east of the tracks. Schools and churches mingled with permanent homes. What had once been a lawless town was now a prospering community.

Folks in fine clothes stared as he and Alice rode by. Hank did not blame them. He and his niece had washed before heading out, but nothing could be done about their trail-worn appearance. The five riderless horses in tow no doubt caused their share of questions, as well.

Hank saw the sheriff's office a short distance from the courthouse.

"Are you certain you want to do this?" Alice asked softly.

Hell no. He wanted to kick the stallion hard and ride out of town like the devil himself was in pursuit. A hard ride would put him over the border into Colorado before a posse could be mustered. He had money and provisions; he could start over. Put all this behind him.

But it would never be behind him; he'd spend the rest of his days running. And he'd never set eyes on Alice, or Nan and her boys, again. The thought saddened him more than he could have imagined a few months ago.

No, he'd see this through. Even if it meant being thrown in a jail cell. "It must be done," he said. He avoided the apprehension in his niece's eyes, made for the sheriff's office. He dismounted at the hitching rail, and Alice did the same.

~~~

Alice had never set foot in a sheriff's office before. It was warm and smelled of sweat and wood polish. A potbelly stove crackled, a coffee pot set off to its edge. At the back wall was a thick door with a small, barred window and a massive lock. Alice realized it must go to the cells, that there may be somebody locked behind it already, and her mouth went dry.

The man sitting at the desk across from her had curly brown hair streaked with gray, and eyes that she guessed didn't miss much. He looked from the window to Uncle Hank, took in his appearance, said, "Are you Henry
~~~

Bonet?"

"I am."

"Bold move, riding into town leading horses belonging to the men who went after you."

"They hunted me, and it didn't end well for them. I'd like to see their horses returned to any family they might have left behind."

"One of them looks to be Nathan Bonet's dun."

"It is. He won't be needing it anymore."

The sheriff stood, his hand moving to rest lightly on the butt of the pistol at his hip. "You here to turn yourself in?"

Uncle Hank lifted his hands away from his body, slow and easy. "I am."

"I'll be taking that sidearm and knife then," the sheriff said. "I don't figure you're here to cause any trouble or you'd have done it by now. Just make sure you hand them over gentle like."

Uncle Hank lifted his pistol from its holster and set it on the desk. Then he pulled the Bowie from its sheath and did the same.

The sheriff stared at the Bowie. "That looks like the knife that killed Tom."

"This knife has never left my side," Uncle Hank said. "If there's another like it, it's a forgery."

The sheriff gave a slow nod. "I figured as much. Nobody around here trusted Tom's brother, least of all me." He pulled in a long, calculating breath. "But that's for the judge to straighten out." He looked at Alice. "And who are you, young lady?"

"Alice Calder." She drew her shoulders back. "This man is my uncle. I – "

"She's here to claim my stallion and possessions," Uncle Hank cut in.

Alice pressed her lips together and remained silent. There was wisdom in silence, she was learning. She could not help herself or her uncle from inside a prison cell, which is no doubt where she'd end up if her uncle hadn't stopped her from confessing to Nathan Bonet's murder.

"Where are you from, Miss Calder?"

"Baker City, Oregon, sir."

The sheriff lifted a brow. "You're a long way from home."

"Yes, sir."

Alice could see he had other questions, but he turned his attention to her uncle. "I have to lock you up, Henry Bonet."

"My niece – "

"Will be looked after," the sheriff said. "You

have my word."

Tears came to Alice's eyes in spite of her resistance. Seeing her uncle led toward that thick barred door scared her. Fear she might fail at freeing him weakened her knees and dread shivered across her shoulders. *What if I never see him again?*

"Alice?"

Uncle Hank had stopped and was looking at her. She saw her own fear reflected in his eyes, but his mouth was set firm and she felt herself doing the same. He nodded, a slight movement but one Alice found reassuring.

"I will be all right," he told her.

~~~

The clang of metal caused Alice to flinch. Keys rattled, then the sheriff came back into the room and locked the thick wooden door behind him. "I s'pect you'll want to stay in town until the trial," he said. "Mrs. Mitchell has a sparc room above the mercantile she lends out. Might be more pleasant than the hotel."

Alice thought of Mrs. Henderson at the mercantile in Baker City and realized she missed the woman. She hoped Mrs. Mitchell was as sturdy. "Thank you," she told the sheriff.

"I'll have someone see to the horses."

"No," Alice said, sharper than intended.
~~~

The idea of someone else tending to Penny and Tracker after all they'd been through together did not set well. Nor did she want anyone touching her uncle's saddlebags. "The stallion's skittish," she explained. "Kindly show me where the livery is and I will take care of them."

The sheriff nodded. "It's at the end of town. You need anything, you let me know. If I'm not here, Deputy Cox will look after you."

"I didn't get your name."

"Sheriff Adams. Bill Adams."

"Good day to you, Sheriff Adams."

He tipped the brim of an imaginary hat. "And to you, Miss Calder."

~~~

Hank heard Alice and the sheriff conversing, but their words were too muffled to make out. He could only hope she was not confessing to the killing of Nathan Bonet. The sheriff seemed a reasonable man, but he was not the one to decide the girl's guilt or innocence. What kind of man was the judge? Would he take into consideration Alice's age and the circumstances in which she acted? Nathan Bonet would have killed her, of that Hank was certain. But would a judge see it that way?
~~~

Hank heard the voices stop and the outside door close. He released his grip on the bars and went to the cot. Alice would do whatever she set her mind to; he no longer had a say in the matter. He no longer had a say in any of it. Until the trial, when he hoped to tell his side of the story, it was out of his hands.

The cot was firm, the blanket clean. He had not rested well at the cabin, haunted by relentless memories. He stretched out and set his thoughts on Wordsworth to settle his mind.

Chapter 19

People bundled in heavy overcoats and wool capes passed by, going about their daily business, talking words that buzzed in Alice's ears. She paid them no mind as she gathered the rope to the string of horses and mounted Penny. Tracker tossed his head, resisted her attempt to lead him away without his rider.

A lump of helplessness swelled in Alice's throat. She didn't want to go either. None of this felt right. She swiped at her eyes with her coat sleeve, saw the sheriff watching through the window. She gave the stallion's lead a tug. "Come on, Tracker. We'll see him again soon."

The stallion settled and consented to follow. A cold wind swept up the street. Alice tipped her hat low against it, shutting herself off from the weather and people and their stares. She was alone. She had learned by now that she could survive fine on her own, but she had no taste for it.

The hostler met her at the open livery door, a man not much taller than herself and almost as thin. His gnarled hands looked like they'd seen a goodly amount of work. Alice dismounted and made provisions for Penny and Tracker and the dun. "Would you see these others find their rightful homes?" she asked.

He squinted at her, then at the horses. "Aye, I can do that. I assume their riders are dead?"

Alice gave a somber nod.

"Mind your back," he cautioned. "There's a handful of kin that won't take charitable to such news."

At the hostler's warning, a cold wind stirred the hay on the livery floor and shivered through Alice. She had not considered herself a possible target, but the man's words held a ring of truth. "Thank you," she said.

She collected the few things from the saddlebags she intended to keep close – the book of Wordsworth, her uncle's secret cache, ammunition, Ma's medicine bag – pulled her Winchester from its scabbard, and paid the hostler. He pocketed the money and set about tending to the horses.

The mercantile was four doors down. A tall, large-boned woman in green calico looked up from behind the counter at Alice's entrance. Her eyes widened. "My heavens, child, where did you come from?"

The woman sounded so much like Mrs. Henderson that tears sprang to Alice's eyes. She blinked them back. "Are you Mrs. Mitchell?"

"I am. And who might you be?"

"Alice Calder. Sheriff Adams said you may have a room to lend."

The woman straightened, the way Alice had seen Mrs. Henderson do so many times when taking charge. "I do. Come in, Miss Calder."

Alice reached into her pocket for payment, but Mrs. Mitchell stopped her with a kind hand. "See if the room is to your liking first, then we'll discuss payment."

The woman led Alice through the back room and up a flight of stairs. The second floor of the mercantile had a tidy kitchen and bright sitting room with two doors flanking it. Mrs. Mitchell opened the door nearest the stairs and stepped inside, motioning for Alice to follow. A double bed, commode and dresser, two chairs arranged around a small table. Lace curtains hung at the window overlooking the street. It was more than Alice had hoped for, and she said as much.

"How long will you be needing it for?" Mrs. Mitchell asked.

"Until after my uncle's trial."

"I see. That was the business you had with the sheriff."

"Yes, ma'am."

"May I ask your uncle's name?"

"Henry Bonet."

Mrs. Mitchell gave a small gasp. "The man accused of murdering Tom Bonet."

Alice's faced hardened. "He didn't do it. He'll prove it at the trial."

The woman looked uncomfortable, like she had something to say but didn't know how to say it. Alice held her gaze and waited.

Finally Mrs. Mitchell said, "Your uncle is half Indian, if I'm not mistaken."

"Arapaho." Alice did not like the way the woman's mouth thinned. "What does that matter?"

"I meant no disrespect," she replied quickly. "Perhaps the sheriff didn't feel it was his place to say anything." Her shoulders straightened and Alice knew the woman felt it her duty to say what the sheriff had not, just as Mrs. Henderson would have done. "I fear the honorable Judge Buckman will not give your uncle a fair trial."

Alice stared at her, lost for words.

"When Charles Buckman was a boy," Mrs. Mitchell explained, "his parents and brother were killed by a band of Sioux. It will not matter to him that your uncle is Arapaho. In the judge's eyes, all Indians are the same and should be on a reservation."

Or in a prison cell. "I am one-quarter Indian," Alice said, her tone defiant.

Mrs. Mitchell's face softened. "I have no quarrel with your people, child. I am a business woman. The color of a person's skin matters not to me, as long as their money is good."

Alice pulled a fistful of coins from her pocket and held them out. "I will need the room for as long as my uncle is in jail," she said. "Whatever the cost."

Mrs. Mitchell refused to take her money. "You will need it to pay for a lawyer. I believe that's the only chance your uncle has of seeing justice done."

"I don't accept charity," Alice stated and continued to hold her money out.

The woman sighed and took a coin, held it up. "For the room." She took a second coin and did the same. "For a bath and new clothes. It won't do to look like a ragamuffin when you call on Mr. Laurence Wolfe."

~~~

Alice did her best to remain grateful as Mrs. Mitchell pulled dress after dress off a rack, held it up to her, "No," hung it up and pulled out another. "This one is lovely," she finally said.

It was green and blue plaid with huge ruffles at the shoulders. Alice curled her lip in spite of herself. "I kinda like the red one," she muttered, even though it was the color she liked more than the dress.

"Oh my, not with your red hair," Mrs. Mitchell declared. She returned the plaid to the rack. "Something less frilly then." She produced a dark blue wool with a broad collar, white cord trim, and four pearl buttons. "This is called a sailor suit."

Alice didn't know anything about the sailor part, but out of all the others she'd seen, it would do. She gave a curt nod.

Mrs. Mitchell smiled. "You'll need shoes."

"Ain't nothing wrong with my boots."

The woman shook her head. "For working
~~~

in a barn perhaps, but not for a young lady who wants to make a good impression."

Resigned, Alice consented. She settled on a pair made of soft black leather and a silly amount of buttons up the sides. Looking at herself in the mirror, wearing a dress – a *sailor suit* – and shoes that pinched her feet, Alice's stomach fluttered. She looked grown up. She could imagine Mrs. Henderson's glee, if she were to see her now.

But it wasn't just the dress that made her look different. The eyes that gazed back at her had seen things, wondrous and brutal. Her features had become firm, unyielding.

When Mrs. Mitchell suggested a new coat, Alice would not have it. "This coat's fine." The woman opened her mouth to put up a fuss. "It belonged to my pa," Alice said, and pulled it to her tight.

Mrs. Mitchell's face softened. "Of course, child." She held out her hand. "Let me wash it for you."

~~~

Pa's coat hadn't smelled this good in a long while. With Mrs. Mitchell's help, her hair was washed and combed into neat braids, her dress and shoes had a new smell about them. She'd taken one look at her stained, tattered hat and
~~~

agreed it was time for a new one. Mrs. Mitchell's mouth pulled in disappointment when she chose a brown English wool with flat crown and wide brim over the frivolous ladies' felts with bows and plumes. Alice saw no sense in wearing something plucked from a bird on her head.

She tried to appreciate the women's smiles and men's courteous nods as she made her way down the boardwalk to Mr. Wolfe's office. There were no sad smiles over the loss of her family, no sneers because of her Arapaho blood, no disapproving looks because she chose to dress in work clothes instead of skirts. No one knew her here. She was just another young lady going about her business. But underneath it all, worry gnawed at her. She'd spent most of her pocket money but still had Uncle Hank's cache. Would it be enough to hire Mr. Wolfe's services?

Mr. Laurence Wolfe was older than Alice expected: thinning white hair, lined face, but trim in a tailored gray suit. He stood as Alice entered, like a gentleman does for a lady in a pretty dress. Alice saw kindness in his eyes. "How may I help you, miss?"

"My name is Alice Calder, sir. I am here on behalf of my uncle, Henry Bonet."

"Bonet. The name sounds familiar."

"My uncle is wanted for the murder of his father, Thomas Bonet."

"Ah, yes. Please," he gestured toward a chair in front of his desk, "have a seat." Alice sat and Mr. Wolfe asked, "Where is your uncle now?"

"Sheriff Adams has him locked up."

"If I recall, Nathan Bonet rode out of Laramie with a posse shortly after his brother's murder to find your uncle."

Alice swallowed hard, her mouth dry. "They're all dead."

Mr. Wolfe's brow lifted. "Perhaps you should start at the beginning, Miss Calder."

~~~

Mr. Wolfe listened quietly as Alice recounted the details of Nathan Bonet showing up in Baker City with a posse, and how it came as a surprise to Uncle Hank that his father had been murdered and he was being framed for it. "I knew he didn't do it right off," she stated, "on account of he'd been living on the Calder ranch at the time of the killing, and he was wearing the knife they say did the deed."

"And where is your uncle's knife now?"

"The sheriff has it," Alice answered. A fact that concerned her, given Sheriff Adams had
~~~

not been upfront about the crooked judge.

When she told him that all the men in the posse were dead by the time she caught up with Nathan Bonet, Mr. Wolfe asked, "You didn't actually see your uncle kill those men?"

"No, sir."

"Did you see him kill Nathan Bonet?"

"No, sir." Uncle Hank's warning stopped her from saying more.

"But you know who did, am I correct?"

Alice remained silent.

Mr. Wolfe pulled in a deep breath and asked, "If I put you on the witness stand to speak on your uncle's behalf and the prosecutor asks you who killed Nathan Bonet, you will be sworn to tell the truth. What will your answer be?"

"I killed him."

Alice saw his skepticism. "And that would be the truth?"

"Yes, sir." Admitting it aloud to a stranger left her feeling empty inside. "He intended me harm, and I stabbed him." Stabbed was too easy a word for what she'd done, the way she sunk the blade of her pa's knife into Nathan Bonet's gut and ripped him open like dressing a deer. Remembering the feel and smell of it made her want to vomit.

"It was self-defense then," Mr. Wolfe said.

Alice swallowed against the lump in her throat and answered, "Yes, sir." She met his stern expression. "Will the sheriff lock me up too?"

"Not if I have a say in the matter. If you wish me to represent you and your uncle, Miss Calder, I will instruct you to speak to no one about details pertaining to the case."

"I understand. What is your fee?"

He said something about a retainer, then, "The final fee will be determined by the length of the case and the outcome. If you have sufficient resources, I can begin today. If you need financial assistance – "

"I don't need nobody's help," Alice stated, though she knew it to be a lie. The retainer alone would take most of what she carried on her. But she refused to be beholding to anybody. She drew her uncle's paper money from her coat pocket and laid in on the desk. "Is this enough to get started?"

"It is." He collected the money, placed it in a drawer and pulled out a tablet. "I'll write you a receipt."

~~~

The lock to the outer door rattled and Hank looked up as Alice strode in carrying a
~~~

covered tray. At least he thought it was Alice, with her long, red braids. She looked more woman than girl in a nice dress and button shoes. Hank wasn't sure how he felt about that. He stood and went to the cell door.

"I brought you supper," she said. "Mrs. Mitchell at the mercantile makes a passable pot roast, but her biscuits are dry." She slid the tray through the slot in the door.

"Thank you." Hank took the tray and set it on the chair. "You've been shopping."

Alice made a face. "It was Mrs. Mitchell's idea. She said it would make a good impression."

"Who were you set out to impress?" Hank asked warily.

She pulled a chair up close to the cell and sat. "Eat your supper before it gets cold, and I'll tell you about it."

She was right concerning the pot roast, thick slabs of it surrounded by potatoes and carrots simmered in the meat's juices. He broke the dry biscuit into the juice to make it more palatable. He was hungry and did not need any coaxing to eat while Alice told him of her meeting with a lawyer, Mr. Wolfe, and the agreement they struck.

"He'll be by in the morning to talk with

you," she said.

"Do you trust him?"

"Can't see that I have much choice, but yes, I trust him."

"How do you plan on paying him?"

"I was thinking of selling the dun, if you're agreeable. He should fetch a couple hundred."

"And that will cover Wolfe's fee?"

She shifted. "It all depends on how long it takes him to convince a jury to set you free. Did the sheriff say anything to you about the judge?"

His niece's question backed a suspicion he'd had, something in the way the sheriff looked at him, as if he had something on his mind but was reluctant, or honor bound, to keep quiet about. Hank had lived long enough and traveled enough miles to know when his Indian blood was going to be an issue. "I want you to go home, Alice, before snow in the mountains makes them impassable." She stood to protest, but he wasn't finished speaking. "You'll need traveling money. Take what you get from the sale of the dun and go back where you belong."

"I ain't goin' anywhere without you!"

"Then you'll watch me hang and be stuck in this godforsaken place until next spring."

Hank would regret the hurt and fear he saw on her face for as long he had left to live. It tore him up to be the cause of it, but he'd not back down from his words. "Please, Alice, for once, do as I say. I don't want something like that to be your last memory of me."

Tears streamed from her eyes and a sob escaped her. It was all Hank could do to keep from crying with her. He wanted to grab the bars of his prison and wrench them from their foundation, escape and take her with him. Helplessness ripped through him like a winter storm.

Finally Alice quieted, wiped her nose on her coat sleeve and pulled her shoulders back. She looked at him steady for long seconds. Then Hank saw her jaw tighten. "No," she said simply, and walked out.

Chapter 20

"I'll collect the tray in the morning," Alice told the sheriff, yanked the door open and stepped out onto the boardwalk. She buttoned her coat against the cold evening air and pushed her hat low on her head. Light shone from the windows of a saloon, men's voices drifting over the lively tune of a piano. Shopkeepers were locking up, readying to go home to their families. She should return to the mercantile, not keep Mrs. Mitchell waiting on her. But her feet did not want to move. Empty grief filled her heart. The only family she had left was locked in a cell and wanted her to go. He'd given up.

Unwilling to face Mrs. Mitchell's questions, Alice decided to check on the horses first. The hostler slept on a cot beside a potbelly stove.

Tracker stood in his stall with his head hanging low, his bottom lip slack in slumber. Penny caught her scent and whickered. Alice tread lightly, let herself into the stall, and buried her fingers in the chestnut's warm side. Penny's skin shivered at the contact; she curled her head to nuzzle Alice's shoulder.

Alice wrapped her arms around Penny's neck, pressed her face close to mask her sobs. Penny stood motionless, a strong shoulder for solace. They had shared many miles and heartaches, Alice and this horse.

When she was cried out, Alice drew back and wiped her face. "Sometimes I think you're all the friend I've got," she said softly.

Penny blinked a big brown eye as if in sympathy. At least that's what Alice wanted to believe. She had a notion to sleep the night in the horse's stall, but feared Mrs. Mitchell would have the whole town searching for her. It's what Mrs. Henderson would do.

She stroked Penny's cheek. "I'll see you tomorrow."

Penny pushed her nose into Alice's chest and caught her off balance in her new shoes. She reached for the stall gate to steady herself. The rattle of the gate latch rousted the livery hostler.

"Who's there?" he demanded.

Alice closed the stall gate behind her and approached. "Sorry to wake you, mister. I was just sayin' goodnight to my horse."

He nodded and sat back on his cot. "Fine then. You have a good evenin'."

"I'll be by tomorrow to discuss selling the dun, if that's all right with you."

"Fine. Fine." He was already pulling the covers back over himself, and Alice left.

~~~

There was a look in Mr. Laurence Wolfe's eyes when he introduced himself and shook Hank's hand through the bars the following morning, one of recognition, yet Hank was certain he'd never met the man before. "Alice tells me she hired you to represent me."

"Yes, she did."

"You and I both know you're wasting your time and her money."

"She believes otherwise," Wolfe said, "as do I." He gestured to the chair. "Mind if I sit?"

Hank nodded. Wolfe pulled the chair close and motioned Hank to do the same. Hank got the idea the lawyer wanted to speak in confidence, out of range of the sheriff's ears, so he sat and leaned forward, resting his elbows on his knees. "Alice needs that money to get
~~~

back to Baker City," he said. "I don't want her spending it on a cause that can't be won."

"From what she's told me, the evidence is there to free you, with the right man to speak on your behalf."

"And that would be you." Hank shook his head. "No offense, but I'm a half-breed in a territory that wants nothing to do with *injuns*. My guilt or innocence means little."

"On the contrary," Wolfe countered. "You are a legal property owner in this county. Your family has history with the people of Laramie."

"What kind of history did Thomas Bonet leave behind?" Hank scoffed. "A drunk who beat his squaw wife and half-breed children."

"He was not always that way."

The lawyer's words drew Hank up short. "You knew him?"

"Not personally. But I heard of the good he did for the local tribes."

Hank sat back, studied Wolfe's expression, the shape of his face beneath skin gone soft with age, the long nose and high cheekbones. The feeling of recognition returned, and he thought he knew its source. "You're a breed," he said, keeping his voice low.

Acknowledgment sparked in the lawyer's eyes. "I am a businessman, Mr. Bonet. I have pledged to serve the people of Laramie."

Red-skinned as well as white. It was left unsaid, but Hank saw it in the man's face.

"Shall we get down to business?" Wolfe asked.

~~~

Hank told Wolfe his story, from staying on at the ranch to help Alice after learning of his sister's death, of hearing some months later that his father had been murdered and that he had been set up as the killer, of being hunted and given no choice but to defend himself.

Wolfe nodded and said his story corroborated the one told to him by Alice, but for one detail. "She said you are not the one who killed Nathan Bonet."

Hank's stomach sank. He looked straight at Wolfe and said, "She's lying."

"I don't believe so. But she's not the one on trial here."

Wolfe paused, and Hank realized that, once again, the man was trying to tell him something without coming right out and saying it. If Alice wasn't on trial, did that mean she wouldn't be charged with Nathan's death? "She's free to go?" Hank asked.

"I will do everything in my power."

Hank knew it was not an idle promise.
~~~

Laurence Wolfe looked a man used to getting his way. To have reached his stature in the community in spite of his mixed blood testified to that fact. While Hank would not allow hope to supersede the hard truths he'd learned through past experiences, he realized this man was his only chance at freedom. He stood and they shook hands.

"I'll be in touch," Wolfe said, and took his leave.

~~~

Mrs. Mitchell gave Alice a new pair of bibbed pants and a blue cotton shirt she got off the boys' rack. "If you're going to wear such things, at least see they fit proper." She handed Alice a package wrapped in brown paper and tied in twine. "I laundered your father's clothes. They're ragged, but there's enough sound material for quilt patches."

Alice thanked her, offered to pay for the outfit, but the woman shook her head and said, "We'll settle your account when you're ready to go."

After breakfast, Alice took a tray to her uncle. She feared he would be angry that she had told Mr. Wolfe of killing Nathan Bonet, but he said nothing when she passed him his breakfast through the bars.
~~~

"Mr. Forman at the livery paid two hundred for the dun," she told him while he ate. "Said it wouldn't be hard to get his money back, given Nathan Bonet had a reputation for treating horse flesh right. He said that was the only good thing the man ever did. Seems people around here didn't think much of him." It didn't make killing him right, by any stretch, but it did ease her conscience a bit, knowing he left no one behind to grieve for him.

"Perhaps that will work in our favor," Uncle Hank commented between bites.

"You talk with Mr. Wolfe?"

"I did."

Alice waited for him to continue, but he just kept eating on Mrs. Mitchell's fried eggs. "Is he going to help?"

"He says he will."

"Good." Alice wanted to feel hopeful, but her uncle's lack of enthusiasm worried her. "It *is* good, right?"

He nodded, sipped his coffee without looking at her.

Alice's impatience got the better of her. "I had to tell him," she blurted.

"I know." Uncle Hank looked at her then, with something like acceptance in his eyes. "Don't ever change on my account," he told her softly, and gave enough of a smile that Alice exhaled in relief. He held out his empty cup. "Is there anymore of that coffee?"

~~~

Two days later, Sheriff Adams strode up to Hank's cell with Mr. Wolfe close behind. "You're free to go," the sheriff said, and unlocked the cell door. "You can collect your things on your way out."

Wolfe stepped forward. "All the charges against you have been dropped," he informed Hank. "The evidence was sufficient to convince Judge Buckman that a trial would be a waste of his time."

Hank suspected Wolfe had played a large part in the convincing. Under different circumstances, he'd have enjoyed watching the man go toe to toe with the judge.

"The other deaths were deemed self-defense," Wolfe continued.

Hank starcd at him. "All of them?"

"Yes." The lawyer smiled. "You're a free man, Henry Bonet."

"There may be folks around these parts who won't take the news well," Sheriff Adams said. "For your own safety, I suggest you leave town as soon as you can get your gear together."
~~~

~~~

The two-hundred dollars Alice fetched for the dun covered Laurence Wolfe's fee with enough left to pay her tab at the mercantile. Mrs. Mitchell looked sad at the news of her leaving, and Alice had to admit she would miss the woman's fussing. Uncle Hank purchased a new set of clothes, which brightened Mrs. Mitchell's mood somewhat. He looked fine in his black broadcloth pants, the Bowie strapped to his leg where it belonged, an ivory shirt, and black overcoat. He politely turned down Mrs. Mitchell's attempt to fit him with a fur derby.

"That's a fine hat, ma'am, but I believe this Montana wide-brim felt better suits my needs." Once he set it on his head, Mrs. Mitchell quickly agreed. The Montana felt fetched a higher price, which Alice was sure helped settle the matter. She liked its red silk band.

Uncle Hank took Mrs. Mitchell's hand in his, not in a handshake but like a gentleman takes a lady's hand. Alice realized at that moment just how handsome her uncle was.

"Thank you kindly for looking after my niece," he said, "and for the thoughtful home-cooked meals."

It surprised Alice to see Mrs. Mitchell's cheeks flush. "You're most welcome, sir. I'm
~~~

pleased things turned out well for you."

Mr. Wolfe agreed to handle the sale of the Bonet ranch, and offered Uncle Hank a loan to cover traveling expenses, using the ranch as collateral. "Once it's sold, I will wire the balance to you in Baker City, minus my ten-percent fee."

Papers were signed and Uncle Hank shook the man's hand. "*Hohóu.*"

"My pleasure, Mr. Bonet."

Alice couldn't decide which astonished her more: that her uncle had thanked the lawyer in Arapaho, or that the lawyer appeared to understand.

Mr. Wolfe winked at her. "It was a pleasure to make your acquaintance, Miss Calder. I hope our paths cross again some day."

"If you ever get to Baker City, I'll set a place at the table," she replied, for she had no intention of ever stepping foot in Laramie again.

It was snowing lightly when they left the lawyer's office. Alice peered up at her uncle from under her hat brim. "If we take the train as far as Promontory, maybe we can get over the mountains before they're snowed in."

He smiled, an ease in his eyes she had not seen in too long. "That's a fine idea."

~~~

The snow was falling fast as Hank and Alice rode from the livery and toward the railroad depot later that afternoon. The air smelled fresh; a surreal stillness had settled over Laramie, as though people were reluctant to venture out and mar the fresh blanket of white with their everyday business. The peace mirrored Hank's feelings. He was a free man.

Alice smiled at him from atop Penny, her eyes bright with joy. She had not given up on him, and they were going home. It fairly made Hank's heart want to burst.

"I've never been on a train," she informed him for the sixth or seventh time.

He laughed. It felt almighty good.

"We should pack a lunch, don't you think? It's gonna be a while before we reach Promontory, and I've seen how prickly you get when you haven't eaten."

Hank chuckled. "As a dried out pine cone, if I recall."

It was Alice's turn to laugh. The sound of it filled the still air. Hank saw a woman and child peer out at them from a shop window. He tipped his hat in greeting. The woman frowned and pulled the child back.

Something about that frown didn't set
~~~

right with Hank. He realized the woman had been dressed in black. A woman in mourning. The sheriff's warning went through his thoughts as the woman in black stepped through the shop door and pointed a revolver at him.

"You murdered my husband!" she cried. Her hand shook as she held the heavy gun out at arm's length.

Hank had never drawn on a woman before. He would regret that later, the hesitation that gave her the first shot. The gun bucked and knocked the woman back a step, the sound deafening.

Even then Hank did not draw but stared at her. "Don't – "

"Uncle?"

Hank looked at Alice. The color was gone from her face and blood seeped through her fingers held to her chest.

Chapter 21

Alice turned in the saddle at the woman's shouted accusation. She saw the gun, saw the smoke from its barrel, felt its sound against her eardrums. Penny skittered. Something punched Alice in the chest and began burning. She looked down at the blood oozing from a hole in the front of her pa's coat. She pressed a hand over it, but it kept bleeding. Her chest hurt something awful, and it was hard to breathe. Uncle Hank kept staring at the woman, unaware.

Fear seized Alice. She didn't have air to speak, but she didn't know what to do, and she didn't want to die. "Uncle?"

He heard her, and the look on his face scared her worse than the pain. From the corner of her eye, Alice saw the woman drop the gun and fall to her knees in the snow. Sheriff Adams was there, held the woman, yelled something Alice couldn't hear because it was getting dark and it was too much trouble to try breathing anymore. She felt herself falling.

~~~

Hank heard the sheriff call for the doctor as Alice's eyes rolled back and her body went limp. He caught her and pulled her onto the palomino with him. The hole in her chest bubbled and he pressed his hand over it even though he knew it made no difference. The few men he'd ever seen shot in the chest had drowned in their own blood. Alice took a bullet intended for him. She would be dead in a matter of minutes, and there was nothing he could do to stop it. A moan started deep in his gut and grew as it clawed its way up his throat.

"Give her to me."

Hank looked down at a clean-cut man about his age, spectacles dotted with snow and riding low on his nose, a black bag sitting at his feet. He had his hands reached out toward Alice.

"I'm Doctor Young," the man said. "Please, I can help her, but there isn't much time."

Hank held onto Alice, unwilling to let her
~~~

die in a stranger's arms.

"You *must* trust me," the doctor implored.

Hank looked at his niece; blood continued to bubble from her chest. *Still alive.* If there was a chance...

He slid her gently into the doctor's arms and dismounted. Doctor Young pressed his hand over Alice's wound and said, "Help me get her to my operating table."

It was but a short distance. A woman wearing a white apron, her light-colored hair pulled back into a knot, ushered them inside. "Lay her there," she said, motioning to a table spread with a clean sheet.

Alice gave a weak groan at being laid flat. "I'm here," Hank told her.

"You'll have to wait in the parlor," the woman informed him, her tone firm but kind. "You're not sterile, and the doctor needs room to work."

Doctor Young had his sleeves rolled up and was washing in a bowl of steaming water. Hank glanced at Alice frail and helpless, most likely dying, on the table. He wanted to tell them to take good care of her, to save her because she was all he had that mattered, but he was too near tears to speak. He nodded and backed out of the room.

~~~

Hank found a chair in the parlor and sat. Light came through the window and cast a beam across the woven rug on the floor. He stared at the colors until they blurred, then shut his eyes and listened. He heard Doctor Young and the woman talking softly in the next room, but could not make out what was said. No sound came from Alice. In the distance, a long, mournful whistle announced the train's arrival at the depot. Hank thought he had never heard a lonelier sound. He and Alice were supposed to be on that train. They were supposed to be heading home today.

The door to the street opened. Hank bolted to his feet and drew. Sheriff Adams raised his hands. "May I have a word with you, Mr. Bonet?"

Hank holstered his gun. "What is it, Sheriff?"

Sheriff Adams lowered his arms and closed the door. "How's Miss Calder doing?"

Hank shook his head. "I haven't heard. The doctor's working on her."

"He's a good man, Doc Young. Educated. Always has his nose in medical journals when he isn't tending patients."

"That's some comfort." Hank sat, his legs
~~~

unwilling to support him any longer. "Join me, if you like."

"Thank you," Sheriff Adams said, "but I just came by to check on the girl, and to let you know I have Mrs. Pierce in custody."

Pierce. The man who caught his stray bullet as he went over the embankment. Nathan had called it a lucky shot. "What will you do with her?" Hank asked.

"That's up to you. Do you want to press charges?"

He should feel rage toward the person who shot Alice, but he did not. A grieving widow who made a poor call in judgment, a child waiting at home. "No. I blame her for none of this."

The sheriff nodded. "She feels deep remorse over her actions, therefore I doubt she'll be of any further trouble. But to be on the safe side, I've confiscated her firearms and will keep them locked up until you and your niece are able to travel."

Hank feared that time may never come. Not if Alice died. He stood and extended his hand. "Thank you, Sheriff."

A short while after Sheriff Adams left, Mrs. Mitchell showed up with a carafe of coffee and a plate of oatmeal cookies. "In case you need a little something to tide you over while you wait," she said.

Her thoughtfulness brought a tightness to his throat. "Thank you, ma'am."

"Would you like me to stay and keep you company?"

"I appreciate the offer, but I believe I'd rather be alone with my thoughts." In truth, he didn't trust himself not to break down in front of the woman.

"I understand." She smoothed the front of her skirt the way he'd seen Nan do so many times. "I'll come by later with fresh coffee."

Hank nodded and saw her to the door. He attempted to pour himself a cup of coffee, but his hand shook so bad he slopped more on the tray than in the cup and gave up. He sat and hung his head.

His thoughts returned to Nan. He wished she were here. She deserved to know of Alice's condition, good or ill. Once there was news from the doctor, he'd send her a telegram.

~~~

Alice woke to pain. It hurt to breathe, like a horse was sitting on her chest. She tried to reach up and push the weight off, but her arms were wrapped tight at her sides by a sheet tucked around her. She struggled to free
~~~

herself, but the pain was too great and she stopped.

A light danced across the ceiling, drew close, and a woman she did not know smiled down at her. "There you are," the woman said softly.

Alice recognized her voice as the one she'd heard in her troubled dream, the one where she was shot and people were shouting all around her. She'd been unable to speak, to tell whoever was carrying her to leave her be because she hurt too much. Then the woman started talking to her, telling her they would take care of her. She couldn't see who it was; her eyes were open, but thick shadows made it difficult to focus, like she was surrounded by ghosts floating over her. They did something to her chest.

Again Alice tried to move her arms, and cried out at feeling trapped.

The woman placed a warm hand on her forehead. "Lie quiet, child. You must not disturb the dressing over your wound."

"Where...?" Alice croaked. Her throat was almighty dry. The air smelled of rubbing alcohol.

"You're in Doctor Young's operating room," the woman explained. "I'm his wife, Lara."

"What happened?"

"The doctor will explain later," Lara said. "Right now, get some rest."

Alice wanted to say more, but Lara's calm, soft voice lulled her eyelids to close. Just for a little while, she told herself.

When next she opened her eyes, it was daylight and Uncle Hank sat at her side, his hand resting on her shoulder. He looked like he hadn't slept, the worry heavy on his face. He gave a tired smile and said, "Good morning."

"You alright?" Alice asked hoarsely.

"I am now."

While Lara wet Alice's dry mouth with a damp cloth, Doctor Young explained about her chest wound and how air got in where it didn't belong. The pressure caused one of her lungs to collapse. By covering the wound with a patch that blocked anymore air from getting in but allowed the air that shouldn't be there to escape, her lung was filling back up and beginning to work like it should. "Is the heaviness in your chest getting better?" he asked.

"Yes, sir. But it still hurts."

He nodded. "It will for a while, I'm afraid. Your body took quite a shock."

"How long?" Alice asked.

"You're young and in otherwise good health," the doctor replied. "If you follow my instructions and get adequate bed rest, you'll be on that train before you know it."

~~~

Hank helped the doctor and his wife settle Alice in a back bedroom. She looked comfortable tucked under a home-stitched blanket, her eyelids already beginning to droop. "I'll let you get some rest," he said, and prepared to leave.

The girl's eyes flew open and she raised a weak arm toward him, grimacing at the pain the effort caused. "Don't go."

Surprised, Hank took her hand. "You're safe here."

Her grip tightened and a tear rolled from the corner of her eye. "What about you?"

She feared for *his* safety, not her own. After all they'd been through, he should have realized it sooner. He heard the doctor slide a chair up behind him. Hank nodded his thanks and sat. "I'm not going anywhere," he told his niece.

~~~

Alice had been asleep for some time when Doctor Young's wife offered to sit with the girl if he needed to stretch.

Hank thanked her. "I won't be long." He located the privy, then he paid a visit to Laurence Wolfe.

"How is the child fairing?" the lawyer asked.

"She's going to make it."

Wolfe released a heavy breath. "That's a relief." He gestured for Hank to take a seat. "How may I help you, Mr. Bonet?"

"Once you've sold my property and taken your cut from the earnings, I'd like you to dispense the balance to the families of the dead men, including Mrs. Pierce."

"As Nathan Bonet's nephew, you're entitled to a share."

"That man was never my family," Hank said, his jaw rigid. "If not for him, I wouldn't be in Laramie, the men who rode with him wouldn't be dead, and Alice wouldn't have taken a bullet intended for me."

Wolfe did not argue. "I'll draw up the papers. Is there anything else?"

Yes, there was. Hank's tone softened. "If something should happen to me, see that Alice's needs are looked after until she is strong enough to return to Oregon."

"You have my word." Wolfe stood and they shook hands. "Have you eaten?"

"Mrs. Mitchell brought me cookies, but – "

Wolfe barked a laugh. "Say no more. Let me buy you breakfast."

~~~

Alice opened her eyes and saw Lara sitting at the bedside, reading a book. Her heart quickened. "Where's my uncle?"

Lara smiled. "He'll be along shortly."

"You don't understand." She attempted to sit up. Pain shot through her chest and she fell back, helpless. "What if somebody tries to kill him and I'm not there?"

Lara stood and pressed a gentle hand to Alice's forehead. "You must lie quiet. The sheriff has dealt with the woman who shot you."

"But there were others," Alice cried. "They have families – "

"Shhh."

"Don't shush me!" Again Alice tried to sit up. She felt the warmth of blood seep from her wound. The pain made her queasy.

A firm hand gripped her shoulder. "Be still." It was Uncle Hank.

Alice sagged into the mattress. "You said you wouldn't leave," she accused through her tears.

"I had matters to tend to." Lara left and
~~~

Uncle Hank sat. "You can't protect me, Alice, any more than I was able to protect you."

"But what if – "

"Life's full of what-ifs. It's like playing poker. You have to play smart and make the most of the hand you're dealt."

"I don't know anything about poker."

"When you're strong enough to sit up, I'll teach you."

~~~

In a few days time, Alice was sitting up, her wound healing to Doctor Young's satisfaction. Hank commenced the poker lessons. She struggled to remember the hand ranks and grew impatient with herself when she lost. "How can two of a kind and three of a kind in the same hand be of less value than four of a kind?" she snapped.

"Four of a kind is harder to come by than a full house." He refused to go easy on her; he knew she would sense it and only become more irritable. He schooled her in a few common cheats. "But don't let me catch you trying any of them."

She did anyway, and riled at herself for being so clumsy at it.

"You can't cheat your way through life," Hank said.
~~~

"Then why show me how?"

"So you can spot when others try to use it against you."

She gave his words a moment of thought. "Like when Pressfield tried to cheat me out of those stocks."

"Yes."

Evenings were the most difficult. "Do you have to go so soon?"

"We both need our rest," Hank reminded her.

He identified with her struggle against helplessness and feeling out of control. She asked daily, "When can we go home?" To her mind, every day they remained in Laramie was another opportunity for someone to kill him. She complained of troublesome dreams and asked for her ma's medicine bag. "There's a sleep tonic in it," she said.

Hank remembered well that tonic. His mother use to make it and insisted he drink the vile stuff when anger made him restless. He brewed a cup for Alice, and with proper sleep came a clearer mind. Almost in spite of her resistance to being an amenable patient, she grew stronger.

And with that strength, Hank saw her self-confidence slowly return.

~~~

In two weeks time, Alice was fit to travel and Hank sent a telegram.

Nan Trevor, Baker City, Oregon.

We are coming home.

Yours,

Henry
~~~

Chapter 22

Alice rested her head against the red plush upholstery and gazed out the train window at the snowy plains. They'd had a thaw in Laramie a week ago, but now the snows had begun anew. The Wallowas were most likely snowed in, but she was confident she and her uncle would find a way through. Her wound was healed over and the bruising yellowed. Doctor Young said she was past the danger of infection. Though still plenty sore, she felt stronger with each passing day and looked forward to being in the saddle again. After four days cooped up in a stock car, Penny and Tracker were no doubt eager to stretch their legs too.

Uncle Hank sat across from her, reading Wordsworth with his eyes closed, his head bobbing to the train's rhythm. He wouldn't admit it, but she saw how the hardships of his own injuries, then hers, had worn on him. He told her about giving the money from the sale of his property to the dead men's families. It was the right thing to do and she admired him for it. When they got back to the Calder ranch, she intended to give him half of her railroad stocks. He could use it to set up his own place, if he had a mind to, maybe settle with a certain widow neighbor.

That would make Jacob and Robert her cousins, she guessed. Robert wouldn't be so bad, but that Jacob surely did get under her skin. She'd find a way to deal with him, for Uncle Hank and Nan's sake.

Alice marveled at the sounds of traveling across country by rail: the forlorn call of the engine's whistle, the chugging of its drivers, the clack of the wheels crossing rail-ends, the hiss and screech of the brakes, then the rumble and creak of the coach car as it rounded a curve. Half a dozen other travelers shared the coach, their low conversations contributing to the mix.

Yet every now and again, a sound that seemed out of place, or a sharp word from one of the passengers, had her looking over her shoulder with a spike of alarm. She reckoned it was something for time to take care of, just like everything else.

The train made frequent stops for fuel and water: Rawlins, Evanston, Green River, and so many more that Alice gave up trying to keep them straight. Some stops were no more than a water tower in the middle of nothing; others offered a place to have a hurried bite to eat. At one stop, she and Uncle Hank bought cheese and crackers and apples to eat on the train. They checked the horses often.

Sudden sheer walls of rock broke into Alice's thoughts and blocked the view on both sides of the coach when the tracks passed through a cut – put there by railroad workers to minimize the elevation change and make the engine's job easier, they were told. Alice felt the train slow as it began the steep grade to Promontory Summit, in Utah Territory, their final stop. At the end of the cut, the view opened onto a vast bluff dusted in white. The train pulled into the depot and the screech of its brakes wakened Uncle Hank. He closed his book and they prepared to disembark for the last time.

~~~

"Horse biscuits!"
~~~

Hank saw Alice drop her saddle in disgust, her hand going to her chest. He had told her it was too heavy for her to be lifting yet, but she needed to find out for herself. She chaffed at relying on his help.

"You did plenty for me," he reminded her. "Allow me to return the favor."

She grudgingly conceded.

Once the horses were saddled, he loaded the provisions they'd purchased at Mrs. Mitchell's mercantile: flour, salt, sugar, beans and rice, dried fruit, a couple slabs of bacon, canned tomatoes. And unbeknownst to Alice, a bar of chocolate, which Hank hid in his coat pocket.

By midday, he and his niece headed north toward the border of Idaho Territory. The muffled quiet of the falling snow was more pronounced after the noise of the train. Hank breathed deep of the fresh air.

Alice tucked like a turtle in the new wool-lined sheepskin coat he had insisted upon before they left Laramie. "Your pa's old coat has outlived its usefulness," he told her. At the long face she made, Mrs. Mitchell stepped in and offered to wash it and salvage what she could for quilt pieces. What remained was in the girl's bedroll, along with the package holding her old clothes. She'd also packed the dark blue dress and button-top shoes.

"I doubt I'll ever have occasion to wear them again," she remarked, "but I didn't want to hurt Mrs. Mitchell's feelings leaving 'em behind."

Hank saw the care with which she folded the dress and was inclined to believe she hadn't found wearing it all that distasteful. But he held his tongue.

They let the horses have their heads for a short while, working the stiffness from their joints. Before long they settled into a slow, easy pace. Hank kept an eye on Alice, mindful of over-tiring her, until she finally snapped, "Quit lookin' at me like I'm gonna break."

He gave a good-natured grunt. "Now who's being prickly?"

It was nice to hear her laugh.

They stopped often, but never for long. On nights when the moon was out, they traveled by its light reflected on the snow. Most nights, they set up camp and did what they could to stay warm, then struck out again at the first hint of dawn.

Four days out, they crossed into Idaho Territory and reached the southern banks of the Snake River. They followed it westward, crossed at Glenn's Ferry three day's later. After a bit of searching, Alice pushed aside a sage, revealing his mother's marker.

The finality of it hit Hank hard. He dropped to his knees, saw Alice step back and allow him to weep in private. *"Biixoo3e3en, Neinoo,"* he said softly, then repeated, "I love you."

They continued to follow the Snake River as it made its way to the Oregon border. Hank killed a mule deer to supplement the provisions. On an evening when they were forced to stop early because of poor light, Alice made a pot of venison stew and skillet biscuits. They ate at the edge of their tarp shelter, where the heat from the fire collected and warmed their backs. The horses rested nearby, under cover of broad fir branches that provided a bit of clear ground and grass to be had.

After Hank and Alice ate their fill, Hank brought out the chocolate bar. "We should eat this before it melts."

Alice blinked. "You been hiding it all this time?"

Hank chuckled. "I knew if I didn't, you'd have it eaten before we left Laramie. I wanted to save it for a special occasion." He unwrapped it as he spoke, broke off half and handed it to her.

Alice started to take a bite, but hesitated. "What's the special occasion?"

Hank shrugged. It wasn't an easy thing for him to talk about. "That we're here," he said, glancing over at her, "enjoying a good meal and a warm fire."

Her eyes filled, and Hank feared he had upset her. Then she smiled, replied, "That's plenty special," and chomped down on the chocolate.

They'd finished most of the bar when she asked, "What day is it?"

"Can't say exactly. We left Promontory on the tenth of December."

She stilled. "It'll nearly be Christmas by the time we get back."

Hank hadn't given it much thought. The holiday often brought more unrest than joy. "What do you want for Christmas, Alice?"

The tears she'd been holding back spilled down her cheeks. It took her a while to answer softly, "I got what I want," she looked over at him, "right here beside me."

Hank swallowed the lump in his throat. "Always."

~~~

When they reached the Oregon border, the
~~~

ferryman in the bearskin coat squinted at them long and hard, then gave a hoot. "I'll be dogged," he declared, "you found your uncle!"

His eyesight may not be all that sharp, but there didn't appear to be anything wrong with his memory. "Yes, sir," Alice replied, "thanks to your help."

The big man slapped his gloves together, his broad smile exposing tobacco-stained teeth. He peered up at Uncle Hank. "You look a might better 'n the last time I saw you, mister."

Uncle Hank chuckled. "Feel a might better too."

"I told the missus I was powerful concerned about you. She'll be tickled to hear you survived. Yes indeed."

~~~

Six days later they reached the foothills of the Wallowas. Alice gazed up at their familiar peaks and felt a sense of home pull at her.

But things had changed, too. Feathery clouds passed overhead, casting their shadows across steep slopes of pine and fir. For all their beauty, Alice knew what secrets lie hidden there. "Come spring, we ought to ride up and bury what's left of those men," she said.

"We will," Uncle Hank replied.

Deep snow forced them to skirt the
~~~

foothills for lower ground. They followed an elk trail through the pines and eventually found a passage that cut off toward the ranch. They crested a low rise and the roof of the barn came into view, then the cabin, the chicken coup and outhouse, all blanketed in white that sparkled in the lowering sun. It was the finest sight Alice had ever laid eyes on.

And yet sadness crept in. She was no longer the naive girl who use to live there, who set out on a stormy night to rescue her uncle like a character in one of Pa's storybooks. She would miss that girl.

An inviting ribbon of smoke rose from the cabin's chimney. Penny's muscles bunched, ready to bust into a run for home. Alice laughed, sharing the feeling, but held the eager filly to a walk.

When they reached the fork to the cabin, a woman stepped out onto the porch and looked in their direction. She wore a thick coat over a blue skirt. Nan's favorite color, just like Ma. Uncle Hank had told Alice about the telegram he sent. She wondered how many days the widow had been showing up at the cabin, keeping a fire going in anticipation.

Alice looked over at her uncle, saw his gaze fixed on the woman looking back at them. "You gonna marry her?"

He drew in a slow, thoughtful breath, exhaled a vapor cloud, and said, "If she'll have me."

Alice smiled to herself. She already knew what Nan's answer would be. But just to tease her uncle a bit, she pulled the carved dog, Lucky, from her pocket. "You might want to hold onto this," she said with a somber face, and held it out to him.

The worried look he shot her was her undoing and she snickered.

His worry turned to good-natured annoyance. He took the carved dog, stuffed it into his coat pocket, and grumbled, "Can't hurt."

Happiness filled Alice near to bursting. She'd been afraid of spending Christmas without family for the first time in her life, but now it looked like she was going to have more family than she could have ever hoped for. "I believe life has dealt us a full house, Uncle."

He flashed her a smile. "That it has, Alice. That it has."

Acknowledgments

Thank you, always, to my talented critique group partners: Kim, Julie, Claudia, and Dion. Your feedback and support are invaluable. Special thanks to Julie for lending her editing skills in the final push to publication. To Gary Dielman at the Baker City Library, my gratitude for sharing from your personal history database, and to the National Historic Oregon Trail Interpretive Center for being such a fabulous resource. To Tina Spencer for sharing her backwoods knowledge and horse ranching sense, and for instructing me on how to dress a deer and bear. Sorry the bear didn't make it into the story! And my heartfelt appreciation to all the friends and family who encouraged me on this project and passed along helpful research material from their own travels.

To Jack, my ideal reader, sounding board, guiding light when things start going astray, awesome designer and tech guy, thank you for being there. My love forever.

About the Author

Writing in the spirit of adventure and happy endings, Pacific Northwest author Cindy Hiday has won numerous honors, including first place in the Kay Snow Awards for Fiction from Willamette Writers. Her humorous literary novel, *Father, Son & Grace* (republished as *Destination Stardust*), is a five-star Readers' Favorite and local book club choice. When she isn't writing, Cindy enjoys growing her own produce, hiking old-growth forests in search of the next waterfall, and strolling long, sandy beaches.